VIGILANTE ANGELS

Book III: The Candidate

Billy DeCarlo

Wild Lake Press, Inc

Hackettstown, NJ

Billy DeCarlo/Wild Lake Press, Inc
P.O. Box 7045, Hackettstown, NJ 07840
billydecarlo.com **(blog, newsletter signup)**

Cover by Archangel Ink http://archangelink.com/
Editing by WordVagabond https://wordvagabond.com/

Vigilante Angels Book III: The Candidate/Billy DeCarlo. -- 1st ed.
ISBN 978-0-9972196-9-2
LCCN: 2017955143

Sign up for the newsletter at billydecarlo.com to stay informed about progress and release dates for new books, audiobooks, and other news.

Order the boxed set or other books in this trilogy at
https://www.amazon.com/gp/product/B073ZLK3TS/ref=series_rw_dp_sw

To all who have suffered through disease or at the hands of others.

For false messiahs and false prophets will arise and perform great signs and wonders, to lead astray, if possible, even the elect.

—MATTHEW 24:24

Contents

1 THE CANDIDATE

THOMAS BRAND WATCHED from his office window above as a woman waited to cross a busy intersection in the relentless downpour. She juggled her umbrella and a grocery bag while holding her child's hand. A driver slowed, motioning her across, and she jumped at the opportunity, hurrying with her son into the street.

Another driver approached from the opposite direction and braked hard at the last second, blaring his horn at them. It startled the woman; she paused briefly in panic, and then pulled her son into a quick trot.

She reached the curb, stumbling as she looked back to ensure her son could negotiate it safely.

As she fell hard to the sidewalk, she released his hand so he wouldn't be pulled down with her. Her bag of groceries spilled onto the wet concrete as her umbrella was blown inside-out and flew out of her grasp. She attempted to regain her feet as her child cried beside her.

Brand erupted in laughter. "Oh, Jesus. I wish I had a video of this shit. Brenda, Harry, come over and check out this elephant wallowing around on the sidewalk. She looks like a hippo at the watering hole on National Geographic. It's priceless."

"Sir, please," Brenda replied. "We've got to focus. The interview is in a few hours. The whole country will be watching, and this network airtime is critical. Please come and sit down so we can rehearse your talking points."

Harry Stinson rose obediently and stood next to Brand at the window. "I hope she's not hurt," he said.

"Come on, Stinson. She's well-padded—a fat fuck like you," Brand said, jabbing the man's arm. "That's some funny shit though, watching fat people fall and try to get up. It's like in the old comedies, before everyone got politically correct, right?"

Stinson didn't answer, and Brand continued. "Check out her kid. Fucking half-and-half. See, this is what I mean. That's why we need to win the nomination and the presidency. We're losing our damn country. We're losing our white identity. The Democrats encourage all this race-mixing, letting the queers run around in the open, and they want to let every filthy immigrant into the country. Anything goes with these liberals."

Brand peered through the rain-splashed glass. "All my hard work to keep my late father's empire smoothly running is what made me a wealthy man. I have to turn over too much of my hard-earned cash to the government just so rabble like that can get a check in the mail every month for doing nothing. I bet that bag of food she just wasted came from food stamps I paid for.

"Stinson, pour me another bourbon."

"Which is why this meeting is so important," Brenda insisted. "Please, let's sit down and do the mock interview. They're going to push you, try to get you to say something controversial so they can make you look bad. Like what you just *said*, for example. You shouldn't be so candid, even in places or among people you believe you can trust."

"I'm not worried about that, not here in my office with you two, anyway." Brand returned to the leather executive chair behind his large, carved maple desk. Stinson placed a full tumbler on the blotter, took a seat next to Brenda, and picked his notepad and pen up from the floor.

"Good," Brenda said. "I'm going to play the interviewer. Harry, jot down anything we should review later, but don't interrupt our flow. We'll go over it point-by-point after we're done. I'll start the machine now." She pressed a button on the recorder.

"Welcome to our viewers. I'm Brenda Mallory with Signal News Network. We're here with Republican presidential candidate Thomas Brand, ahead of the widely anticipated Republican primary debate. Sir, welcome."

"Thank you, Brenda. I'm a big fan of your network, but I say that to all the networks, and I despise all of them. I can't wait to be president and shut down the media like they did in Russia. I'm also a big fan of your lovely ass and big tits." He laughed again, slapping his desk, and Stinson followed suit until a glare from Brenda shut them down.

"If we're not going to be serious, I'm out of here," she said angrily. "Or better yet, I'll insist that your wife sit in on these meetings."

"Alright, alright. Can't we have a little fun while we're doing all this boring shit?" Brand picked up a remote control and turned on a large television hanging from the opposite wall. "Let's see what they're saying about me today. That's more important than playing these stupid games."

2 DOMINGO

TOMMY DOMINGO SCRATCHED his thick white beard. He considered shaving it to relieve the constant itching, but didn't want to risk being identified. He lay down on the bed in his sparse bungalow. An ocean breeze blew through the windows, pleasantly cooling the sweat on his skin. It was too hot and humid for Whitey to join him as he typically did, so the dog gazed at him from the cool tile floor in the bathroom.

He reflected on his decision to abruptly leave his doctors, chemo treatments, and cheating wife behind to spend the remainder of his time quietly alone in the Keys. *And I missed my son's funeral. My poor Bobby.*

"I guess we had no choice, Whitey. No sense in waiting around for them to figure out I killed that corrupt cop and show up to bust me. I do miss Nurse Carmen, though. It's just you and me now, and this ain't a bad place to die.

"This is the life Bobby wanted. He and I should be here together. He just wanted to ditch the rat race and be a guy on the sidewalk making spray-paint art. Why the hell do people spend their lives sitting in traffic and shoveling snow, when they could live somewhere like here? Why did I, come to think of it?"

He rose, went into the kitchen, and filled Whitey's water dish with fresh, cool water from the tap, then scraped the remains of a can of dog food into his food bowl. He unscrewed the cap of a large orange prescription bottle and took one of the pills inside, washing it down with a handful of water. He inspected the label. *Forbaxatel. Take with food.* "We're both almost out of the grub we brought with us, buddy. I guess we better finally venture out of here to restock."

He went to the rust-speckled refrigerator and removed a large bottle of wine, holding it up to the window to inspect its level. "More importantly, we're almost out of vino." He tipped the bottle up and guzzled a large quantity. "Fruit of the vine, Whitey. A gift from God...or whoever."

Whitey ran from the bathroom to the kitchen for his treasure as Tommy moved to a rattan couch in the living room. He sat on its thin, flimsy cushions with his bottle and turned on the television. He leaned forward to adjust the antenna, bringing the picture into focus just as the evening news was beginning.

Tommy reached beneath the couch and pulled out a tin cigar box. Pulling the lid off with a metallic pop, he examined the layers of cellophane bags neatly rolled inside. He lifted it to his nose, closed his eyes and inhaled. "Oh damn, Whitey. Why did I ever waste so much time smoking cigs when this stuff was available? Thank you, Moses, for the stash. Rest in peace, my friend."

He tried to place it on the coffee table and misjudged, spilling the box onto the floor. As he picked up the tin to refill it, he noticed a folded paper in the bottom. He pulled it out and read it carefully.

Friend Tommy,

We talked a lot in the chemo ward about being able to die on our own terms, so I wanted to give you a parting gift. I put this in your stash box before you left so that you'd find it when you probably need it most— when your marijuana was almost gone. You only need one, but I left you two, just in case you screw it up and lose or break one. Take it straight for a more immediate effect, or dilute it if you wish. I hope you never need to use it, but I know if the time comes, you'll want it, as I'm sure I will also.

Your friend,

Sensei Molletier

He searched the floor, picking up the rolled bags of pot and putting them back into the cigar box. When he had replaced them all, he slid off the couch slowly, grunting with the effort. On his knees, he searched again, this time spotting two small black vials beneath the coffee table. He retrieved them and sat back on the couch, turning them over in his hand. They had identical white labels with Korean lettering.

The news anchor had moved on to coverage of the presidential primaries. "The surprising rise of West Virginia businessman Thomas Brand to one of the top three Republican candidates has gotten the country's attention. His far-right views have served as a divisive factor within the party and across the nation."

The scene cut to a Brand campaign rally, where a large crowd of fired-up supporters raised their fists and cheered at everything the candidate said from his pulpit on the stage. A large banner that read "Brand Brigade" was held above a group of men and women. The banner featured a Confederate flag on one side of the lettering, and "White Power" with a clenched fist on the other. Some in the group sported Nazi symbols. *How many of our people died fighting that garbage, and now this closet racist stands for it?*

The candidate was railing against the scourge of homosexuality that he claimed was poisoning society's values. Tommy thought of his gentle son and what he must have endured during his life because of homophobes like Brand, not to mention the corrupt cop, Carson, who had caused Bobby's death.

At that moment, he saw the root of all of the evil that had tortured and tormented less fortunate people like his son and his late African-American friend Moses for their entire lives. People like Brand, who lavished themselves with riches, gorging on the fruits of their wealth with no sense of charity, viewing those less fortunate with disdain. *I'd like to cut the head off that evil snake.*

A black protester had been detected near the front of the audience by the candidate, who then urged the crowd to remove him. The camera zoomed in to show the man being hustled toward the exit by large security guards. He was shoved and spit on by the people under the banner as he passed them.

Tommy felt his anger grow and began talking to the screen. "Fucking morons. C'mon people—this guy's a con artist. Use your brain. He won't follow through on these promises to you. All he's ever done is screw people over. Don't be duped." He took another large swig from the bottle.

"Damn good thing this guy's got a snowball's chance in hell of making it through the next few primaries, Whitey. But if he ever did get elected, God help us all."

The effect of the booze, medication, and stress began to gnaw at his stomach as he watched. He turned the TV off and went to the kitchen to prepare his dinner. He opened a can of stew and dumped it into a small pot, which was still crusted with the remnants of his lunch.

He took his wine and meal outside to a rustic, weather-worn picnic table that sat in a small clearing behind the house. Whitey followed and took his position beneath the table at his master's feet. "Sorry guy, you're not going to want any of this crap," Tommy said to him. "Yours is probably better. Maybe we should both eat that and save money."

As he sat at the table eating, his mind flashed back to dinners at his own kitchen table a long time ago when Bobby was small. They'd recap their day, tease each other, and look forward with excitement to what they would watch on television together that night after the boy's homework was done. Those were happy times, and revisiting them made him morose. *I can't ever go back home. Bobby's dead. Margie was unfaithful. It won't ever be the same.*

He finished his meal and pulled a joint and lighter from his shirt pocket. As he smoked it and the drug's effects mixed with the wine, he enjoyed the quiet surroundings. He stood and surveyed the area, pleased that there were no other cabins visible through the dense vegetation and mangroves along the nearby channel. *No neighbors and plenty of escape routes, perfect.* His thoughts turned to the events that had brought him to this place.

The news footage of the black protester being treated so disrespectfully still bothered him. His friendship with Moses had helped him understand what it really meant to be in the minority in a country full of people who hated anyone who was different from themselves. *Not one of them considers for a moment what it would be like to be hated by others your entire life.*

He felt a wave of sadness and remorse as he recalled how Moses had died while assassinating the pedophile priest they'd stalked together. *You went rogue and left me behind to save me, Mos. I'm still a little mad, but at least you denied cancer the chance to take you out. I miss you, buddy.*

He reached beneath his shirt and cradled the St. Michael medallion that Moses had given him. *The archangel, vigilante, warrior.*

The disappointment of not helping Moses execute the priest was erased by the thrill he felt at the memory of looking down at the remaining pulp of Carson's disfigured body and taunting him as his life slipped away.

But I promised to spend my last days for the common good, to make the world a better place, and that one was only personal.

That brought him back to the images and words of Brand's campaign. The man stood for everything Tommy hated, and reminded him too much of everything that he used to hate about himself. The thought of what would happen to so many unfortunate people if the man ever got elected terrified him. *I guess I won't have to worry about it though; I'll be gone.*

Whitey rose and put his front paws on Tommy's knees, looking at him expectantly. Tommy picked the dog up and placed him on his lap. Whitey rolled over, and Tommy rubbed his stomach. "Okay, pal. Let's grab some cash and see if we can figure out how to get to that farmer's market I saw from the taxi on the way in."

Placing the dog on the ground, he shuffled slowly back into the bungalow. He pulled the blinds in the bedroom and pushed the nightstand aside. Using his pocketknife, he pried up two floorboards and retrieved a few twenty-dollar bills from one of the wrapped stacks below.

After putting everything back the way it was, he grabbed his knotted, gnarled walking stick from the door handle and left the cabin with Whitey, taking care to lock the door behind him.

3 TARA

TARA HUMMED AND SWAYED to the music flowing from the overhead speakers as she arranged colorful organic vegetables into woven wooden baskets. Her long, gauzy tie-dyed dress felt good as it grazed her legs.

"How're you doing down there, Ol' Jerry?" She crouched to ruffle the Irish Setter's graying hair.

She glanced up at the canopy over her stall in the farmer's market, thankful for its protection from the heat. She stopped to pull her gray hair back into a ponytail, then moved to a basin to wash her hands and went back to her task.

Her favorite song came on, and she began to sing along with it softly. "Sugar Magnolia..."

Movement through the shimmering heat far down the road caught her eye, and she stopped to see what it was. It had been a slow day, as it always was when it was abnormally hot. She focused and saw a white-bearded man with a walking stick making his way toward the market. A small white dog kept pace by his side. He marched toward the market with a slow, determined gait.

She went back to her sorting and singing, lost in thought until a voice startled her.

"Hello," the man said. "Where's the frozen food at? I think I want to climb into the freezer."

She turned to face him and smiled. "It's a tough walk in this heat, no matter how far. Come on in here, under the shade."

She went to the wash basin and poured water into a bowl for his dog, then to the prep table. She cut a large slice of dark red watermelon and handed it to the man. "This'll help. No frozen food here, only good stuff. I'm Tara."

The man took the melon with one hand and shook her offered hand with the other. "Tommy. Tommy B..." He stopped for a moment and shook his head. "Just Tommy."

She smiled at him. "Then I'm Just Tara. Good enough. What can I do for you, Just Tommy?"

"I'm new here. Just retired. When I noticed that my collection of memorial cards was growing, I figured why not move to paradise before I get my own?

"Anyway, I need to stock up on a few things—some grub for Whitey and me here, to start with. Got any cans of dogfood?"

Tara measured him before responding, taking note of the sweat rolling down his face and his soaked white V-neck t-shirt. He was still breathing hard, though trying to hide it, and smelled faintly of alcohol. Her intuition signaled a kind soul, but someone with secrets and the weight of the world on his shoulders. A tough exterior belying a sensitive nature. *Another one who's come here to run from the world. I wonder how long this one will last.*

She pulled a folding chair for him from against the wall and set it up, then grabbed an ice-cold bottle of water from her cooler and handed it to him.

"Tell you what, Just Tommy. I could use some company. How about taking a break and hanging out for a while? Those two are getting acquainted." She nodded toward the two dogs. Whitey was circling and sniffing Ol' Jerry, who lay still on the floor, disinterested.

"Ol' Jerry here is getting on in years, not much energy these days," she continued.

Tommy took the seat. "That makes two of us," he said. "Thank you, Tara. I can't stay long, though. I just need to stock up on some things."

"Listen, Just Tommy. You can probably tell I'm an old hippie, if the Grateful Dead tunes and tie-dye weren't your first clues. Our bodies are our temples, and the same goes for our beloved companions. Can I get you something much better than that garbage they put in cans for your little friend here?"

"Whitey," Tommy reminded her. "Yeah, sure."

"I make it myself. All natural." She pulled a container from a shelf and scooped out a spoonful of its contents, offering it to Whitey, who eagerly devoured it. "Looks like Whitey's a fan," she said.

"Works for me. I'll take enough for both of us," Tommy said. "Probably better than the crap I've been eating."

Tara laughed. "I bet it is. I can fix that too, though. Everything here is organic. What kinds of fruits and veggies do you like, Just Tommy?"

Tommy looked around. "About everything. I'm not too picky, but I'm not much of a cook. I'm a real sick guy, so it doesn't much matter what I put into my body now. It's about run out its usefulness."

Tara detected a slight slur in his speech and wondered if it was from the illness or the alcohol. She took a seat next to him and placed her hand on his knee. "Tommy, I'm a big believer that no matter what your challenges are, they can be helped significantly with the right frame of mind and what you put into your body. You're not the first person to lose hope and come here to get away from everyone and everything."

Tommy shifted uncomfortably. "How do you know that about me?"

"I'm good at reading people. I see the goodness in you, and the sadness. This part of the key isn't exactly a tourist area. It's mainly people like us, who want to stay off the grid as much as possible. Fishermen, loners, and locals."

"Sounds like my kind of place," Tommy said.

"Alright then, Just Tommy. How about I box you up a week's worth of stuff that you can easily make into meals? It'll be on the house—we'll call it a sample pack. If you like it, I'll see you every week for refills. Then I'll have you on the hook and jack the price way up. What do you like?"

Tommy considered the offer. "I'm a big pasta guy…"

"Right on, then. I happen to have some fresh homemade pasta and some jars of marinade made from local tomatoes and spices. It'll be easy for you to make. I'll fix you right up. All my stuff is from the local farms and restaurants."

She moved around her stall, filling a cardboard box with provisions, again singing along to her music.

"You sing nice, Tara," he said. "I need two more things. I'd like some fresh fish to cook up, and where's the liquor store around here?"

She stopped and stood in front of him, hands on hips. Her voice took on a motherly tone. "Just Tommy. Didn't you hear my lecture about our bodies as a temple? A drunk temple doesn't do a man much good. It's poison."

"Yeah, well," Tommy said. "Maybe you didn't hear me when I said I was on a short runway. Nothing matters much anymore for me, anyway."

She sensed that she'd crossed a line and angered him. "To each his own; live and let live. If you decide you want to change that, let me know. In another lifetime I was a nurse, and I did a lot of work helping folks with substance problems. If that's your choice, I respect it."

She watched him as he seemed to be considering her offer. *It's got him, but he wants to change.*

"Thanks. I'll keep it in mind. Funny thing—I didn't touch the stuff for a long time, until just lately. At first, it helped kill a lot of pain. Now it's turning into the pain. Like it was back when I had a problem with it."

She was happy that he was opening up to her. That was a good first step. "That's what it does. It's evil. I'm here for you if you need me, Tommy. I also lead a tai chi group on the beach a few times a week. At sunrise, if you want to join us."

"I'm trying to keep a low profile, but I'll think about it. I know a guy who has a black belt."

She laughed. "No, not like that. Tai chi doesn't have belts. It started as a martial art, but today it's used as a very slow-motion, spiritual form of exercise. It's very popular with old farts like us."

Tommy looked up at her, finally with a hint of playfulness on his face. "Hey. Speak for yourself. I'm only forty, it's just been a rough forty years."

They laughed together. "And listen," Tara said. "If it helps you get away from that poison, I have some other, more natural ways to relax and catch a nice buzz."

"Now that I'll take you up on. My stash is going to run out at some point, and I like it a lot more than the booze."

She brought the full box of provisions and placed it on a table in front of him. "To answer your earlier question, my friend Micco has a fish stall a few booths down. He's a fisherman, so it's all his own fresh-caught stuff. Go visit him, then come back for the box. I'll keep it chilled for you. I'm not helping you with the other problem though, buddy."

"Geez. A real hard-ass teetotaler hippie. Only I could run into someone like that," Tommy said, rising. "Alright. I'll be back shortly, Tara."

4 FISHMONGER

TOMMY MADE HIS WAY past the stalls of the farmer's market with Whitey padding along faithfully by his side. He passed a stall selling Asian specialties and peeked inside. The mystical appearance of the bottled and packaged goods on the shelves and the dank, exotic smell of incense and herbs brought him back to the old Korean shop he'd visited with Sensei Molletier. The stall was empty of patrons, and an old woman wearing a large conical hat sat in the rear, under the shade of its canopy. He entered and approached her.

"Excuse me, mama-*san*. Do you speak English?" he asked.

She looked at him with contempt. "This is America, why the hell wouldn't I speak English?" she asked.

Tommy was embarrassed for his gaffe. "I'm sorry..." he started to say.

"Vietnam vet, right?" she asked. "You're not in Saigon anymore, G.I."

"Yeah, okay. Got it. I'm sorry, again. Excuse me, but can I ask where you're from?" Tommy asked.

"Manhattan," she said, looking at him defiantly.

"No, I mean, like what country," he tried again.

"United States. Manhattan's in New York City."

Tommy paused, exasperated. *She's good. And I'm an idiot.* "Okay, point taken. Let me try again. I'm sorry, ma'am. Old habits die hard, but I assure you I don't mean to insult you. I'm just an old man, and I'm not thinking right. I'm sick, and the damn sun has fried my brain. I'll try again. Can you tell me what your heritage is?"

She leaned back, satisfied. "That's better. My people are from Korea."

"Oh, good," Tommy said. He reached into a pocket of his cargo shorts and pulled out a small black vial. "Can you tell me what this says?"

She took the vial from him and examined it. "It'll cost you ten dollars for translation service," she said.

"Oh, for chrissakes, lady," Tommy said, fishing in his rear pocket for his wallet.

"Take it easy, GI Joe. Just fucking with you. It says, 'Death with Dignity.' Where did you get that? It's poison. Something that was given to our spies in the Korean War in case they were captured. Very deadly. You better handle it carefully."

"Wow. A friend gave it to me. I mean...I found it."

She looked at him doubtfully, then reached behind her to a shelf and pulled a straw farmer's hat similar to her own from a stack. "Here, wear this before you do fry whatever brains you have left. Ten bucks."

Tommy took it and examined it. He liked that it could help shield his appearance. "Not a bad idea. Deal." He thought for a moment, examining the shop wares. "So…you got any rice wine?"

She paused before responding. "This ain't a damn liquor store. Need a license for that kind of thing." She eyed him, then said after an uncomfortable pause, "Wait here."

She got up and went into a curtained-off back area of the stall, returning after a few minutes with a bottle wrapped in a brown paper bag. She held it, looking at him. "Hold on. You a cop? You look like a cop."

The question took Tommy by surprise. *What the hell, is everyone around here psychic?* He looked at the bottle, and it called to him. He felt the urge, the hunger for a drink. It upset him, and he felt weak and hated himself for wanting it. He fought to just walk away, but he couldn't. The force of it had grown and was now stronger than his will. "No. I'm not a cop. I'm just a sick old drunk. I came here to die."

Now she now appeared sympathetic and held the bottle out. "I can't sell it to you. No license. It's a gift."

Tommy smiled at her gratefully. "Thanks. Thank you so much." He took it and shoved it into the larger pocket on the side of his pants. *I guess it was all an act. What a nice lady.*

"The hat's twenty bucks now," she said, crossing her arms.

"Oh, Jesus." Tommy pulled his wallet out and paid her. "Well, thanks," he said. He placed the hat on his head and made his way out of the store with Whitey following.

"Get well soon, papa-*san*," she called out after him.

He made his way past more stalls, feeling a little foolish wearing the conical hat, but thankful for its relief from the hot sun. He smelled the fish as he approached a row of refrigerated display cases. Cleaned fish fillets were lined up neatly on beds of ice. Whitey sniffed excitedly and put his front paws up on the displays, trying desperately to see the contents.

A man emerged from the shade of the back of the stall. Tommy took note of his high cheekbones, and jet-black hair pulled into a neat ponytail. He wore a clean white smock and a bone choker made of polished conch and coral which contrasted against his dark, red-hued skin.

"Can I help you, sir?" the man asked Tommy.

"Yeah, what's the catch of the day?"

"Grouper, yellowtail snapper, and blackfin tuna. All caught this morning."

"I'll take some of the tuna. Two fillets, please."

Tommy watched as the man expertly wrapped the fish in paper. "I don't mean to offend, but are you some kind of Indian?" Tommy asked the man hesitantly. "I mean, Native American."

"No offense. I'm proud of my heritage. I'm Seminole. My ancestors are from here, but there aren't many of us left in the area. The government packed most of us up and shipped us to a reservation in Oklahoma after the Seminole wars in the mid-1800s. My name's Holata Micco. It means 'Alligator Chief.' I'm named after the leader of the third Seminole wars. People just call me Micco, though."

He placed the wrapped fish in a small insulated box with ice and handed it to Tommy.

"I'm Tommy. Tara sent me. She's a real nice lady," Tommy said as he paid and shook the man's hand.

"She's the best," Micco said. "She's kind of the leader of the people in our small community. We all go to her for help solving our problems or mediating issues with each other. We don't have a police force. Never needed one. She's wise, like a shaman."

"No police—that's a good thing," Tommy laughed. *Real good for me, being a fugitive and all. In fact, an important criteria.*

Tommy made his way back to Tara's stall.

She saw him coming and smiled. "Well, well. Look at you, Just Tommy. I see you found Mrs. Park. Nice hat!"

"Hey, you're not supposed to recognize me in this disguise," Tommy responded. "Who's this Just Tommy you speak of? I'm Mr. Just Incognito."

They both laughed. Tara brought his box of provisions from the cooler and sat it back on the counter. She pointed at the wrapped bottle protruding from his pocket. "How the hell did you find something to drink around here?" she asked.

"We all have our secrets, Tara," he answered sheepishly. "Yeah, I know, I know. Save the lecture. I'm going to work on it, I promise. I just need to get settled in. Moving is stressful."

"I'll hold you to that. I'm a patient woman. Listen, it's gonna be a long haul back down that road in this heat with all this stuff. Let me give you a lift. I'll use Micco's truck. It's community property, more or less. He leaves the keys in it for anyone who needs it."

"You kidding?" he answered. "I'm a Marine vet. This is nothing compared to all the crap we had to carry through the jungle back in 'Nam. Although that was pretty long ago."

"Yeah, yeah. I know you're a tough guy. You have it written all over you. But you don't strike me as a dumb tough guy."

He hesitated, thinking he'd already broken his vow to not get to know anyone or provide information about his past, and not wanting to disclose his location. He relied on his instinct to trust her. *I'll have her drop me at a decoy location nearby.* "I guess so. Hard to turn down a ride from a pretty lady, especially in this heat."

"Joe," she called to the man in the next stall. "I'm gonna give this guy a lift. Can you watch my booth for a few minutes?" She led Tommy to the pickup, and he climbed in with his package and Whitey.

They drove with the windows down, the deep blue ocean speckled with white-crested waves on their left. Whitey sat on Tommy's lap, tongue out, head in the window, with the wind blowing back his ears. Tara was humming along with the CD that was playing. Tommy glanced over at her, enjoying her attractive profile. *I guess we're about the same age.*

He thought about how he'd tried to make love to Nurse Carmen and failed. *Humiliating. I'm not going through that again. Besides, I came here to die, not fall in love.*

"I do some surfing, you should join me sometime," she said, breaking the silence.

"Ha. Thanks, but if one wave hit me I'd break apart like those toy crash-up cars they used to sell. Remember? The ones that you would run into the wall and they'd break into a bunch of pieces?"

"I don't think you're giving yourself enough credit, Just Tommy. Think strong, and you'll be strong. The mind sends signals to the body. That's why positivity is so important. Anyway, maybe just come out to get in some beach time and watch. You could save me if a shark comes. You seem like the heroic type."

"I used to be, Tara," he said. "Used to be, in another life. This is good enough," he said to her, pointing to the side of the road.

She scanned ahead. "You sure?" she asked. "I don't see a driveway."

"It's close enough. I'm a bit set back from the road."

"Alright. I catch your drift, man of mystery. I respect that. You sure you're okay with this load?"

"Sure am," Tommy responded. "I'm gonna make one of those Alaskan sleds, but with wheels. Whitey here will be my sled dog." He realized he'd given himself an alias, but had forgotten about the dog. *Hopefully it won't matter.*

She laughed, and he loved its musical, genuine quality. They smiled at one another as he closed the truck door.

"Don't be a stranger, Just Tommy," she called to him as she pulled away.

5 THE INTERVIEW

BRENDA SAT AT THE FAR END of a long conference table, across from Brand, who was holding court. The seats were filled with older, snow-haired white men in expensive business suits. She was the only woman.

"Stinson!" Brand yelled. "Damn it, I told you not to let my glass sit empty."

His executive assistant jumped nervously and darted to a crystal decanter on a nearby stand, using it to fill Brand's glass.

Brenda considered holding her tongue, but decided to speak up. "Sir, we've got a lot to cover. Maybe take it easy on that stuff for a bit."

"Keep your place, Brenda," he snarled. "If I didn't know how much these old bastards appreciate the eye candy, I'd boot you out of this meeting right now."

She felt her face flush with embarrassment and anger. She considered quitting as campaign manager once again, but her stubborn nature prevailed, as always. *I hate you, you filthy drunk fucker, but I need this win for my career. The campaign manager for a miracle win, if we can pull it off.*

"Alright," Brand addressed the group. "This started as more or less a publicity stunt, free advertising for my businesses, and to fuck with those idiot Democrats. None of us realized that there's a real appetite for change out there and that the public would rise up and love me." He paused, as if wanting the words to linger with the group.

"Now," he continued, "things have changed. We actually have a shot at this. Imagine that! All of you, the top business leaders in the country, have a huge opportunity. If we get in, we can do so much: slash corporate and personal tax rates in the highest brackets, kill all of the damn environmental regulations that cut into our profits. Not to mention shipping out all of the immigrants coming in who don't even speak English, and get rid of these damn entitlement programs that have half the country sucking on the teat of the government. That's where all our fucking tax money goes."

Brenda listened and thought about her sister, who had been born handicapped and relied on assistance, unable to function normally throughout her life. And her brother, who at his lowest point had nothing, but was rescued by government-sponsored clinics that helped him beat his addiction.

"Except we all know that with the loopholes we have now, we don't pay much in corporate or personal taxes," one of the oldest of the group said. The others laughed uproariously, and Brand joined them, holding up his tumbler in salute.

Brenda glanced up from her notepad at the man who had spoken. Like Brand, his cheeks and nose were a ruddy red, covered by burst blood vessels. *Another alcoholic heart attack waiting to happen,* she thought.

"Damn right," Brand said. "Thanks to the past Republican administration. But if we fuck this up, and the Democrats win, you can kiss all that goodbye. They'll shitcan the whole works. It'll be handout after handout, and people will get lazy and not want to work."

The group murmured in agreement.

You all got everything handed to you, born with silver spoons in your mouths, and you still worked, Brenda thought.

Brand continued. "So, we have to soldier on and escalate our strategy. We'll keep the churches in our pocket with our anti-queer talking points: AIDS, gay marriage, etc. We keep the middle class in our pocket by continuing to tell them that we'll cut their taxes and that we'll create all kinds of jobs with the tax breaks we're giving ourselves.

"We keep the old people on board with the anti-immigrant spiel—maintain the fear factor. They're all convinced immigrants are pouring over the border with backpacks full of drugs, aiming to rape and pillage them. We keep those goddamn hillbillies onboard, too. What the hell do they call themselves? Brand Boys?"

"Brand Brigade," Brenda interjected.

"Right, Brand Brigade. Now that's a scary bunch of dumb rednecks. But they're *my* dumb rednecks. Which reminds me—Brenda, at the last rally that fat bastard in overalls bear-hugged me. The crowd loved it, but he smelled to holy hell. Don't let that happen again."

"You have to stop breaking protocol and going into the crowd, sir," she reminded him.

He ignored her. "Where was I? Right—the hillbillies. We keep up the military talk, strong America, kick-ass, U-S-A chanting and how we're going to drain the swamp of these corrupt politicians because we're outsiders. In their jaundiced eyes, we're businessmen—respectable, successful men of action. That keeps them onboard. Somehow, they associate our money with brains, even though I know that's not the case with many of you," he said with a smirk.

"And what about after we win?" another man asked. "How are we going to follow through on all of those promises?"

Brand stared at him, and the group waited in anticipation. "Who the hell cares? After we win, we do whatever the hell we want."

The group treated Brand to another round of laughter.

"If we keep our standing with those groups until election day, we're in. President Brand—can you believe that?" he said proudly, waiting for the group to salute him.

They did, with a round of applause. The stereotypes revolted Brenda, who thought about how challenging it had been to raise her kids on her own, watching the executives she'd worked for throughout her career shower themselves with excessive compensation out of corporate profits while denying her and other mid- and low-level workers pay raises and bonuses.

She looked around at these men whom she knew to the last one had been born into entitled families, never having to struggle or want for anything. She felt the urge to get up and scream at them, but then thought of her kids, and how they depended on her and her career for their chance at a better life. *Hopefully, a better life than I had.*

"Brenda! Pay attention, damn it," Brand shouted, startling her back to the reality of what was happening in the room.

"Can you go see what's holding up the refreshments? The guys here haven't had a chance to watch you walk across the room in a while." He looked at the group. Most of them knew it was wrong to laugh at the comment and did not, although some couldn't resist doing so to please him

"Back to my point," Brand continued. The country wants someone tough. That's me, folks. And don't forget one thing—as President I'll have full pardon powers. So those of you who are currently under SEC investigation for your 'financial creativeness,' and those who haven't been caught yet..." He paused for their uncomfortable laughter. "That means it's open season. I'm very forgiving in these matters."

She got up in disgust, wishing they all knew about how he had dodged the draft with his father's political donations. How he couldn't tolerate even the smallest amount of pain or discomfort. How he was completely and secretly owned by the bourbon he consumed throughout the day and night. *He's a functional drunk right now, but sooner or later it'll cost him dearly.*

"To get to the closer," Brand said, "this is where you men come in. We need to step up the war chest. Bigger donations. We need more ads, more rallies, more visibility. We're still behind in the polls. The rest of the Republicans take us seriously now, and they're fighting back. Let's finish strong, win this nomination and the presidency, and then I'll take care of each and every one of you. You can take it to the bank, so to speak."

She wondered how anyone in the room could actually believe him, given that he'd just laid out a plan to deceive the entire country. She knew he would do the same to them. She wished the men knew just how much of their donations he was secretly laundering into his own private accounts. She thought of the absurdity of the fact that he had just insulted their intelligence, then asked for money, and gotten away with it.

Am I really going to be a part of unleashing this horrible man on our country? How will I feel about myself for the rest of my life? How will history judge me?

6 BEACH BUM

THE WARM SAND FELT GOOD on Tommy's feet. He buried them in it and then lifted them back out, feeling the grains run between his toes as if he were a human hourglass.

The sound of the waves crashing and rushing to the shoreline, accompanied by the backing group of seagulls, the feel of the ocean breeze, the sun on his damaged body, and the tangy salt air all made him feel alive again.

It brought him back to the many years he'd spent on the beach as a kid. *Coney Island.* He closed his eyes and laid back on his green wool military blanket to imagine it, using the power of his mind to play the memories back. It was easy, because the background sound was still the same. He saw his mother, fussing over them all. His father presided over them in his beach chair, wearing Bermuda shorts, a white wifebeater, black socks and shoes, drinking beer after beer from a dented green metal Coleman cooler. He imagined the sound of the lifeguards' whistles and the smell of suntan lotion.

He remembered the continuous stream of gleeful noise from the boardwalk that had been nearby. The swoosh and rush of the coaster and screams of its occupants. The joyful calliope sound of the carousel, and the smiles on the children riding its painted horses. The incredible, delectable sight, smell, and taste of the lightly greased hot dogs spinning slowly on steel rollers, and funnel cakes dusted with a snow-cropping of powdered sugar.

He wished he could open his eyes and find himself back then. *So many things I would do differently.* The thoughts made him happy, in fact euphoric, a rare thing for him these past years. His thoughts slid to the years when he'd recreated those childhood memories with his own little family—him, Margie, and Bobby at the same beach, enjoying the same things. Amazingly, it had changed little during the time between his own childhood and his son's.

He tipped up the brown paper bag that held his bottle of wine and drained the last of it. He felt drowsy and disoriented from the alcohol, and regretted that it was dampening his enjoyment of the otherwise relaxing day.

The memory of little Bobby began to turn his mood sour. It brought him to his own failing as a parent—his refusal to acknowledge or accept Bobby's homosexuality until too late. *Until just before he died.* He thought back in anger at the corrupt cop who had caused Bobby's death. He gratified himself by replaying his gruesome execution of Detective Carson, before leaving to come to the Keys to run out his last days and die alone.

His peace was interrupted by a family nearby. They'd been enjoying the beach as well, adding to the typical noise of kids squealing from the scary waves and cool water, and as such, they had blended into the day. They were packing up to leave, and the kids weren't on board with the plan. The oldest was complaining loudly, and the youngest was sitting in the sand crying.

Tommy noticed the beer cans littering their area, and that both of the parents appeared to be intoxicated, stumbling around haphazardly while trying to pack up towels, blankets, and beach toys. The father struggled with the umbrella, attempting to close it while facing against the wind, resulting in it fighting back against his efforts.

These can't be locals. Must be rogue tourists. Tommy struggled to his feet. "Need help?" he asked, walking toward them. The man didn't answer, continuing his battle against the umbrella.

"Here, turn around facing this way," Tommy motioned to him.

The family stopped what they were doing to watch, and the man glared at him as he spun in the direction Tommy indicated. A gust of wind snapped the umbrella closed and pinched his fingers.

"Motherfucker!" he exclaimed. "Mind your own fucking business, pal. Now look what you did," he said to Tommy.

"Excuse me, I don't think you should talk that way in front of the kids," Tommy said.

"You should mind your business, mister," the wife chimed in weakly, slurring, as if afraid not to defend her husband.

"Okay, okay. Just trying to help is all. Forget it," Tommy said.

His apology apparently wasn't good enough for the man. He dropped the umbrella, shaking his hand out, and approached Tommy menacingly. He came forward as far as his beer gut would allow, until their noses were inches from one another.

"Let it go," Tommy urged him in a low voice. "Your kids are watching. Let it go for your children."

"Screw you, old-timer," the man leered. "You embarrassed me in front of them."

"Kick his ass, Dad," the older boy urged.

Jesus Christ, Tommy thought. "C'mon, buddy. It's a beautiful day. Let's all go about our business here." He worried about his recent lack of strength and cursed the disorientation that the bottle of wine had brought him.

"Go ahead, Dad," the boy called again. "Fuck him up."

"You shush," his mother admonished him without taking her eyes off the men, looking hopeful that there would be an altercation.

The man smiled and grabbed Tommy's shirt.

Tommy stepped to the side and grabbed the man's wrist in his own iron grip. He twisted the man's arm behind him, turning him to face his family and forcing him down to his knees. He gave a final shove, and the man face-planted in the sand.

Tommy walked back toward his blanket and watched warily as the man got up. The man faced him and shouted, "You're lucky you're old. I just can't kick an old man's ass. Got to teach my boys here about respecting elders. Lucky for you, grandpa."

"You're a drunk," Tommy replied. "Both of you. You should be ashamed, as parents."

The woman stepped forward this time. "What the hell are you talking about? I've been watching you sit there and drink from that paper bag all day, you damn wino."

Tommy's addled mind slipped back a little. "I don't drink..." he started to say, before remembering. *Now I do. She's right—I'm no different from them. How did I come to this?*

"Let's get out of here. This sumbitch is crazy," the father said. They began to move down the beach, leaving behind the beer cans and other trash.

"Hey," Tommy called out. "What about your trash?"

"How about you get that for us, pal," the man called out to him.

The seagulls had already moved in. Tommy made his way to the trash, scattering them in his wake. As he cleaned up the mess, a thought struck him. *I'm not winded from that. I didn't get winded walking here. Walking to the market wasn't too bad, either. I feel stronger, somehow.*

He recalled Dr. Mason's words about the trial drug he had stolen before his getaway. *It also seems to rejuvenate some patients.* He felt under his ribs for the liver pain, which had been so persistent that he'd learned to ignore it. Mason had confirmed that the cancer was swelling the organ.

It's gone. No pain. Holy shit. The stuff is working.

Tommy was overjoyed at his revelation. Whitey seemed to understand as well. Tommy picked up a piece of driftwood and threw it. Whitey bounded to it and brought it back and they repeated the exercise until the dog was worn out.

"Ha, can't keep up with the old guy, huh, Whitey?" Tommy taunted.

They began the walk off the beach, and Tommy whistled as Whitey trotted happily beside him. As he always did on their long walks through the channels and mangroves near the cabin, Tommy said, "Let's go home, Whitey." The dog took his cue and led the way to the bungalow.

7 LOST IN PLACE

THE AROMA OF THE TUNA grilling over charcoal was appealing to Tommy, but downright intoxicating to Whitey, who danced around the grill on his hind legs in anticipation. Tommy brushed on the olive oil that Tara had included in his provisions and sprinkled the fillet with spices. As it cooked, he tossed together a salad from the veggies she'd selected for him.

He'd spent the day elated, continually probing around his body in amazement that the places which had always caused him pain no longer hurt. He and Whitey had hiked through the surrounding area that morning, and he was no more winded than a reasonably fit man in his sixties should be.

For the first time in a very long time, he was genuinely happy.

As he sat at the picnic table with his meal, he fed bites of tuna to the dog.

"What do you think, Whitey? Maybe this is some kind of miracle drug. Maybe we have a longer runway than we thought. We can get a nice long stretch of time here. Maybe help out over at the farmer's market. Maybe find a nice girl. I think I already know one."

The dog looked at him quizzically, waiting for the next morsel.

"I'm tempted to cook the other fillet. Maybe for dinner, eh?"

Whitey seemed to understand, rising up and putting his paws on Tommy's knees.

"What a day, huh kid? What a great day. Maybe we should celebrate."

He had made it that far into the day without drinking, feeling invigorated from the hike and thrilled at the thought that the cancer might be on the run. At the thought of a new lease on life, or perhaps at least a longer one. At the idea of love. Tara's words and her profile, the chance of her, had kept his pangs of desire for the booze in check, but it was only mid-afternoon.

"Let's go inside and watch some TV," he said. He picked up his plate, dish, and silverware and headed into the cabin, the white dog following obediently behind.

After he'd cleaned the dishes, he turned on the television and settled onto the couch. Whitey leaped up and nestled against him. Tommy opened the stash box and prepared a joint, returning the vial he'd been carrying to its mate in the box.

"I guess we won't be needing you, Mr. Death with Dignity. Not for a while anyway. Good old Molletier, always looking out for me." He remembered that Molletier had taken a share of the Forbaxatel. *Damn, he's probably getting better too. I hope it's working for him like it is for me. Good for you, Sensei.*

"You know what, Whitey? We have one bottle of that 20/20 bum wine left. Might as well do away with it, and be done with the drinking for good, so it won't tempt me later. We're starting a new lease on life tomorrow. Today, we celebrate and then close the book on the drinking chapter."

The dog looked at him apprehensively, as if it understood that his logic was questionable.

Tommy went to the bedroom and retrieved his gun case and the bottle from his under-floor hiding spot. The bottle felt good in his hand and smelled heavenly as he twisted off the cap and drank in the aroma.

His body tingled down to his loins in anticipation of the first sip, and then he took it—a long one. It brought relief, but deep down he knew he should be feeling the opposite. Knowing it was the wrong decision, he made another promise that it would be the last time.

As darkness fell, he smoked, drank, and watched a mindless sitcom while waiting for the evening news. He went through the robotic litany of cleaning his semi-automatic handgun as his thoughts again took him over.

This is the kind of show that Bobby always watched. The thought of his son took him back again. *I failed him. That poor kid. He was never free. Never able to be himself. I rejected him. Didn't want to hear it. I should've protected him. He died, my partner on the beat died, and Moses died. I wasn't there for any of them. What kind of person am I? Margie, too—she would never acknowledge Bobby's homosexuality. No matter how hard he tried to open up to us.*

The thought of his estranged wife angered him. He realized that rather than his usual mellow high, the pot was bringing him down. He didn't allow himself to blame the alcohol. The thoughts and memories served as fuel to that fire.

Margie. The 'good wife,' I used to call her. Bullshit. Screwing my partner Paulie and then screwing my brother-in-law. A damn cheating drunk is all she was.

His anger was growing, boiling up inside of him. Anger at the past, anger at himself for being weak. It was too late now, he'd already betrayed himself. He thought about Tara and felt that he had betrayed her too, by drinking. *Another person I've let down. She's too good for me. Just like Carmen.*

The thought caused him to attack the bottle harder. The news finally came on and moved immediately to coverage of the Republicans' star candidate, Thomas Brand.

"We have insider information on candidate Brand. Sources within the campaign have hinted at a drinking problem, saying that Brand has a weakness for good bourbon, and it often interferes with his demeanor and decision-making."

Great, he's a fucking drunk on top of everything else. Just what we need, a drunk with the nuclear codes.

A supporter from the Brand Brigade was being interviewed. The reporter asked what she thought about the latest revelation.

"I think it's just fine," the woman said. "Who are we to talk? Most of us like to drink too. It just shows he's a regular guy like us, despite being wealthy. A regular Joe. One of the people. That's why we love him. He's the kind of man I'd like to have a beer with."

Jesus Christ. That's the same bullshit logic that got the last knucklehead elected. Look where that got us. Tommy tipped the bottle up to enjoy another slug but found it empty. He looked at it with surprise, then pointed the bottom up toward the ceiling again, shaking it over his open mouth to get the last drops. He forced his tongue into the neck as far as it would go, then angrily threw it across the room. He heard the glass break within the paper bag when it hit the wall, and decided to let it lay. Whitey yelped at the noise and jumped down to inspect the bottle, but Tommy called him back to his lap.

Clips from Brand's rally that day were being shown. Brand was spewing his typical vitriol against gays and immigrants to chants from a raucous crowd. "No-Ho-Mos. No-Ho-Mos." Tommy watched the footage of the candidate, who wore a pleased smile. He picked up the reassembled weapon and pointed it at the man's forehead. "I'm out here, motherfucker. Your worst nightmare. You better not push me too far, or...pow," he said as the man continued his hateful rant. Tommy continued to sight down the barrel until tears began to cloud his vision. He closed his eyes, becoming angrier as he listened, until a sudden explosion jolted him.

Without realizing it, he had placed his finger on the trigger, rather than in the standard safety position alongside it. It was a measure that had been burned into him his entire career—gun safety 101. Whitey bolted from the couch, upset and crying, and ran to the bedroom to hide under the bed. Brand continued ranting on the television. *And, to top it off, I fucking missed. Thankfully for the TV, I guess.*

He put the gun down and went to his dog. When he finally coaxed him out from beneath the bed, Whitey was shaking violently and looking at him with sad, confused eyes.

"I'm sorry, Whitey. I'm so sorry," he repeated, stroking the dog and holding him close to his chest. *I'm on a roll. There's yet another better soul that I've let down and fucked up.* When the dog had calmed, he inspected the wall until he found the bullet hole and slug embedded in the pine. *Hit a stud, at least.*

He peered out of the window and imagined sirens and flashing red-and-blue lights in the distance. The pot and booze fueled his paranoia. *What if they do come?*

"We gotta go, Whitey! We gotta go, quick!" He jumped up, replaced the pot in his hiding place and stuffed the gun into his waistband, taking care to set the safety this time. He imagined the sirens coming closer, imagined light in the distance toward the road. He scooped up the dog, turned off the television and lights, and ran out into the woods surrounding his bungalow.

He panicked, thinking about the police asking for his identification, possibly recognizing it was fake, finding out his real identity, and extraditing him back home, to spend the rest of his newly extended life in prison. *Just like Moses was afraid of. He was right. A cop in jail is not a good thing.*

He splashed through the channel and stumbled through the mangroves and brush in the darkness, terrified. Branches whipped his face, and briars tore at his legs as he used both arms to shield the dog, unable to protect himself. He continued until he'd covered a considerable distance, ignoring the searing pain.

Stopping to listen, he sat to catch his breath. The dog crouched at his feet, looking confused and scared. He leaned back against a tree, Whitey nestled on his gut and fell asleep.

Sometime later, the dog shifted, startling him. It was still dark, and he reasoned that it couldn't be that much later because his mind was still clouded from the effects of the pot and wine. Paranoia crept in again as he began to worry about the gators that he knew frequented the area. He stood and let Whitey down to relieve himself under his watch. He patted his firearm, still tucked into his waistband.

He picked the dog up and attempted to find his way back. Trying to retrace his steps, he became confused. He tried to assess how long and how far he had run from the bungalow. They walked endlessly in the dark, amid strange noises. "We're lost, Whitey. Completely fucking lost out here."

He was hungry and sick; still drunk but with the beginning of a hangover making its presence known. He began to trot, then stopped to vomit, shielding the dog. A loud rustling noise from behind him evoked images of predators stalking them. Panic set in, and he began to run again, aimlessly in the dark.

As fatigue started to overtake him once more, he tried to duck a limb at the last moment and stumbled, losing his balance. He crashed to the ground, turning himself on his back on the way down so as not to crush his beloved companion.

8 THE CANDIDATE RISES

BRENDA LEAFED THROUGH press clippings from each of the major city newspapers, highlighting key passages. She knew they were going to make Brand angry, but he'd be angrier if she tried to sugar-coat the truth. *It is what it is, Mr. Brand. I'll save the best for last, to end the meeting on a high note.*

She reluctantly gathered the stack of papers and headed toward the elevator, deciding to take a less robust approach with him. *Why do I bother? Sometimes I almost hope he loses. I can't take the drama or insults much longer. I hope he's not loaded yet.*

As she arrived on Brand's exclusive floor, she approached his admin assistant at the desk outside the office doors.

"Dear Leader awaits your presence," he said, rolling his eyes. They shook their heads at each other.

The assistant leaned toward her on her way past. "I took a poll. There is actually nobody working for this man that doesn't despise him. Including his wife."

"Thanks for the laugh. I'm going to need it after Brand sees these," she said, waving the stack of clippings at him.

Brand was reclining in his leather executive chair with his shoes off and argyle-socked feet on the desk. He held a remote control in one hand and a large tumbler of bourbon in the other. She waited as he continuously rewound and replayed a section of his last rally.

"Damn, Brenda. Look at me. Has anyone ever looked more presidential?"

She didn't answer, thinking it was a rhetorical question, until she realized he was waiting for a response. "No, sir. That is one of your finest moments to date. You get better every time."

"Thank you, Brenda," he said, taking a large swallow. "Tell me what you liked the most about that one."

She hesitated. "I guess just the crowd's reaction, they were really into it."

He put the tumbler down. "Brenda, the crowd is a response to *me*. I was asking about *me*, Brenda. Not the crowd. Jesus."

"Oh, of course. I think it's the suit. You look great in it. Presidential."

"I give up," he said, picking the tumbler back up. "Okay, let's get through this. I want to catch the next political show at the top of the hour."

They went through the editorials, which primarily consisted of damning and dire predictions of what his election would mean, and thankfulness that his odds of winning the Republican nomination were slim. Some were insulting, and he began to drink more quickly as his temper grew.

"The fucking press is full of goddamn liberals and Jews. I'm going to do something about that as soon as I'm elected."

"Sir, the country is built upon a free press. It's a fundamental pillar of our democracy. If you try to tear it down, it would be bad for you."

"Bullshit. Don't give me that crap about what the founding brothers or whatever they were called said hundreds of years ago. Maybe the press was fair then. They're all a bunch of god-damn socialist commies now. They don't understand my greatness. I can't seem to get it across to them.

"I mean, look at this rally," he continued, gesturing to the TV with the remote. "The place was mobbed. Sold out. Lines of people waiting down the street to get in."

"Yes, but all in all, that's a fraction of the people who live in that city alone. You can't be led to overconfidence by those crowds. It will cost our win. We have to behave as if we're behind." She was tempted to tell him that most were there for the freak show his events had become.

He brushed her comment off. "What's coming up? We need more events—maybe something for cops and veterans. I can't stand either group, frankly. They put on a uniform to impress the women, stand around doing nothing their whole career, then want a big pity party and attention everywhere they go. One or two do something heroic, and the whole bunch of them want the damn credit for it. What the hell do they make, a few thousand a year? They're nowhere near as successful as I've been.

"But everybody loves them, so I have to love them. Or at least pretend to, for now. If we somehow win the primaries this week, we can lock up the nomination. Once we do that, I want a big event with lots of vets and cops surrounding me to kick off our run in the general election. Start setting it up. I feel good about this."

She sensed he was intoxicated past the point of no return, and she wanted badly to leave. As she had planned, she finished with some articles from extreme right-wing publications, which were very favorable toward him. It brightened his mood, and as she knew he would, he switched to his flirtatious demeanor.

"Hey, Brenda. There's so much stress with all this work every single day. Here we are again, working late. I'm all knotted up from the stress. Would you mind?" he asked, motioning to his back.

"No, I'm not giving you a back rub. Ask your wife."

"She's out of town. Again. You know how it is with us. It's pretty much for appearance, she hates my guts. I'm bored of her, too. I'm gonna be on the market someday. Until then, we could keep it on the down-low. You and I could be good together."

She began picking up her things without answering.

"You want a drink, Brenda? How about dinner? I could have it brought up for us. The best stuff. You name it—steak, lobster, whatever you want. Let's just have dinner and a few drinks."

"I can't, sir. I won't. Please don't ask again."

As he always did, he began to sulk.

I've got to get out of here, now. Brenda was heading for the door when she remembered a promise she'd made. She paused, torn between that promise and the door. They were heading out of town for events soon, so she had to ask.

"Sir, my mom's a fan of yours. She's pretty old and not doing well—early stages of Alzheimer's. I want to do something for her while I can since I'm away a lot. Do you think you could meet her if I brought her up here before our trip to Miami?"

He swiveled in his chair and turned to her, red-faced from the booze. "Uh, you know how I am with the germs and all that." He opened a desk drawer and pulled out an eight-by-ten black and white photograph of himself and signed it with a flourish, not bothering to ask her mother's name to add it. He held it up, enticing her to come closer to him.

I knew he'd do that. You can't catch Alzheimer's, asshole. She approached the front of the desk, rather than come around behind it as he was indicating. She held out her hand for it, and he gave it to her with a grudging look.

"Thank you," she said, as she went straight for the door without looking back. "See you tomorrow."

He didn't answer.

9 WALK IN THE WOODS

TOMMY WOKE TO A THROBBING head and Whitey licking his face, whimpering. He reached up to push the dog away, and his hand came away wet. He held it out, expecting to see the dog's saliva, but found it coated in blood instead. Lying on his back, he looked straight up at the trees rising into the dim early dawn sky, struggling to piece together what had led to him wake up there.

He recalled a peaceful, beautiful morning full of optimism and joy at his unexpected good health. A hike. Happiness. The rest came slowly. *Tuna. Weed. Booze. Brand. Bobby. Anger. Gunshot. Stupid.*

He attempted to rise, but pain forced him back down. Pain—everywhere. He reached behind his head and found a knot, more blood, and the protruding layer of shale he must've hit when he fell. The urge for a drink came, to kill the pain, and he cursed it and then himself.

He pulled himself up slowly—first on his elbows, then his hands. He resisted the urge to lie back down and sleep, instead pushing himself up to a seated position. Whitey circled him, whining and confused.

His legs were scratched deeply from the briars, as were his arms. He could only imagine his face was the same or worse. He became conscious that he was itching all over, and looked closer to see the welts from insect bites, a few guests still feeding on him. He swatted them in frustration, and they swarmed noisily around him, seeming to realize he was weakened prey, taunting him.

What kind of loser gets a second chance at life and fucks it up like this? What am I doing here? This isn't paradise. It's hell. All gone: Bobby, Moses, my wife, my life. I'm still on borrowed time. What do I have to live for, exactly?

He wished he had kept one of the vials on him, as he'd planned to. *Death with Dignity. Not so much, out here like this.* He saw his gun lying near-by. His rib cage complained greatly as he reached for it, but he stretched, ignoring the pain, and pulled it into his grasp. He glared at it accusingly, looking for something else to blame for the circumstances he found himself in. *Nobody's fault but your own, pal. Loser.*

He swatted at the bugs again, waving the gun around, and felt himself spiral mentally out of control. Whitey had wandered off, leaving him all alone. *All is lost. I have no home, no friends. I've lived a long life...Fuck it.*

Racking the gun to clear the chamber and load a fresh round, he popped the safety off. He laid back down with his head against the rock, again closing his eyes to everything but the pain in his mind and body, and pressed the barrel of the gun against the side of his head. His hand shook for want of a drink. This time, he held his trigger finger alongside, rather than around the trigger. *If you're going to do it, you better be sure.*

He let his hand fall to rest on the ground and thought of the irony of escaping the jungles of Vietnam to die alone in the swamps of the Florida Keys. *The big, bad vigilante takes himself out like a coward. I'm my own next victim. By my own hand. A coward's way out, as they say.*

He ran through the reasons for and against. He remembered the peace that Moses seemed to have after the last thread of hope disappeared for him in the doctor's office that day. The man seemed to finally be at rest and excited to find the answers to life's greatest mysteries. The idea of joining Moses and his son appealed to Tommy considerably—the idea of finding peace even more. *They're in heaven, but the Good Book says I can't go if I kill myself...*

He fought off the excuses and again pushed the barrel of the gun against his head, this time with his finger wrapped around the trigger.

Tears rolled from the corners of his eyes, down the side of his face, and into his ears as he gripped the gun and tried to find the courage to end his misery. *Come on, it won't even hurt unless you screw this up too.* He decided to count it down.

"Five...four...three...two..."

Whitey bounded up between Tommy's out-spread legs and lay on his stomach, his face on Tommy's chest. Tommy opened his eyes and looked at the dog's sad eyes. *Oh hell, who's going to take care of you, Whitey? You're gator-bait out here in the swamp.*

He thought maybe he'd wait, see if he could place Whitey with Tara first. *Tara.* Just thinking her name made him feel a little better. He felt beneath his shirt for the St. Michael medallion that Moses had given him and thought about how disappointed the man would be if he gave up here. *And I'd have to put up with him nagging me about it for eternity. He was brave, he didn't quit until the priest was dead, no matter how sick he was at the end. He was heroic. Like I want to be.*

He picked himself up, leaves and twigs falling away from him as he rose. The sun had also risen, and as his thinking cleared, his attitude became more confident. *How can I find my way back?* The solution came to him. He placed the dog on the ground and said, "Let's go home, Whitey."

The dog glanced at him and then began to lead the way. Joy began to creep back into Tommy's heart at the thought of being back in the cabin, safe. He still held some fear that the cops could be there waiting, though. *I'll take my chances, at this point. I want to go home.*

He struggled to keep pace with the dog, or at least keep him in sight. Whitey happily jumped over stumps and occasionally stopped to roll on the ground, allowing Tommy a chance to catch up. Finally, the surroundings became familiar to him. He called to the dog and picked him up.

"You saved us, buddy. Thank you, Whitey. You saved me. You sure did."

He hugged Whitey, who happily licked his neck. They covered the last distance to the cabin cautiously, Tommy looking for any sign that someone might be present, or might've been there. He approached from the back, creeping at a crouch to the rear window, and peered in.

It all looked the same as he had left it. He let the dog down went around to the front and entered. The bottle still lay on the floor in the paper bag. He went to it and picked it up.

"I'm done with you. That's it. No more. Time to suck it up; toughen up. You aren't beating me," he said to the crushed mess. He took it to the trash and threw it in. *I want every day to be just like the first half of yesterday was. I'm going to make it happen. I'm a goddamn Marine.*

He fed the dog and refilled his water dish, then went to the bath and filled the tub with scalding water. He stopped to look at himself in the mirror. His face was scratched and caked with blood. White streaks were traced out from his eyes where the tears had washed the mess away. *I'll never get to this condition again. Ever.*

He removed his clothing and put the firearm away, then eased into the tub slowly. It was incredibly painful getting in, but as soon as he was immersed, it was heavenly. He lay still for a while to enjoy it and put his head back to think. Then he slowly began scrubbing himself clean.

10 TAI CHI

T HE DAYS PASSED SLOWLY. Not wanting to go back to the market until he had
healed, Tommy stretched out their provisions as best he could. *I look like a damn swamp
monster—or something the swamp monster ate and
spit out.*

He acknowledged the other reason he was
avoiding the market. He knew that once there,
he'd be tempted to visit Mrs. Park's stall and pick
up another bottle of rice wine. Or worse, find his
way to a liquor store.

He passed the time with his dog, shaking and
trembling from the time he woke until he was
able to finally drift off to sleep. He kept the TV
off, its content too upsetting and in itself a re-
minder of that horrible night. He lay on the bed

for long stretches, alternately closing his eyes and replaying his life, and staring at the ceiling above in thought about what his limited future could be.

Whitey remained faithfully by his side. The warmth of another body, another loving form of life, was welcome to Tommy and a tremendous boost to his spirit. "You're getting me through this, Whitey. I know you're doing your best, my friend."

He found a few books of classic literature in the dusty drawers of the cabin's furniture and read them. They were the first books he had read since his adolescence, and he welcomed the ability to lose himself in other worlds, to take his mind off his own problems and revel in the happy endings of others. *There won't be a happy ending for me, that much is for sure.*

They went for increasingly long walks each day, and he was sure to never miss a dose of the Forbaxatel. One morning he rose early and looked at his face in the bathroom mirror. The wounds had healed. Examining the rest of his body as he showered, he was pleased with the results.

He dressed in loose, casual clothing and called to his companion. "C'mon, Whitey. Let's head to the beach for the sunrise." He placed his Asian farmer's hat on his head, and for the first time, he left his walking stick behind.

They made their way down the path to the secluded beach. Tommy hummed and talked to the small dog, carrying a blanket and towel. As the beach came into view, he saw a small group standing in loose formation. A woman stood before them, looking elegant in a thin see-through coverup over a bikini. Tommy stopped to watch as she moved slowly, gracefully, arching her body and limbs as the group mimicked her. *Tara.* They were silent, accompanied only by the rush of waves and cheering gulls. It was an incredibly peaceful scene. They all seemed to have the kind of serenity he yearned for.

Tara bent at her waist and swooned sideways until she was facing him, and their eyes locked. She smiled and jerked her head at him to join them. He made a shrugging motion to her as if to say he didn't know how to do this, and she worked a sweeping gesture into her routine to summon him to the back of the group. *This isn't exactly keeping a low profile, but what the hell.*

He walked toward them and they all silently smiled in welcome. Dropping his things, he took up a position in the rear of the group. He watched Tara move in graceful beauty, trying to copy the moves and feeling foolish, even as her smiles and nods encouraged him. His body was stiff and aching from the ordeal it had been through in the last two years, and particularly the last week.

It got easier; he became less awkward, and he started to feel some of the peace he hoped it would bring to his soul. Whitey watched with interest, getting up occasionally to chase a gull that had come too close.

The group finished the session and, surprisingly, didn't socialize with each other. They seemed to give each other space, packing up their things and moving on silently, but Tommy sensed their spirit of camaraderie. *Tight-knit locals, all minding their own business. I could get used to this.*

He spread out his blanket and sat. After the rest of the group had gone, Tara approached.

"Mind if I join you, Just Tommy?"

He patted the blanket next to him. "Sure thing. That was fun. Incredibly relaxing. Just my speed, too—slow-motion."

"Well then, we look forward to seeing more of you. Less than thirty minutes is all you really need. Gets the head in the right place to take on whatever else comes your way until it's time to hit the sack."

"Wow," Tommy replied. "Where were you the last sixty-three years of my life?"

She responded to his flirting with another smile. "Don't look back, Just Tommy. Only look forward. Learn from your mistakes to make the future a better place. Take those lessons forward, and always move on as a smarter and better person. You can't change the past, you can only make the future better because of it. No matter how bad it was."

He took that as an invitation to open up, and tried to resist the temptation. *She can't help with anything that happened, but she's right.*

"It's not that easy with some things," he said. "Take me, for example. I've been fighting the big

C. It's been a war. You always know it's right behind you and coming for you, no matter what you do. You do what you can—chemo, pills, throw furniture in the way to slow it down, but it's still coming, no matter what you do. It's relentless."

He realized he was downbeat. "I got some new medicine though, a trial drug called Forbaxatel. It seems to have rejuvenated me, somehow. It feels like my cancer just disappeared."

"That's great!" she exclaimed. "Where are you going for treatment around here, though? All the way back to Miami? Those clinical trials have to be monitored."

He knew he'd said too much, and didn't want to lie to her. "I'd rather not talk about it, Tara. I don't want to be rude. It can't last forever—I'm kind of here to run out my time."

She put her arm around him and hugged him. She smelled earthy and clean, despite the thin layer of perspiration they both wore.

"Let's go for a swim," she said. "Race you!"

She stood and removed the cover-up, then the bikini top, trotting to the shoreline, and entering the blue water between waves. It seemed as if he were watching a movie. *Bo Derek wishes she could look like that at her age. She's amazing.*

She implored him to join her, swimming further out past the breakers.

"Well, Whitey. I guess I'm going swimming," Tommy said. He rolled up the legs of his drawstring linen pants and waded out until he was up to his knees, then dove into the next wave.

The water running over his body as he swam below the surface invigorated him. He held his breath while his lungs fought for air, determined to reach Tara. As he did, he grabbed her calf and then let go, surfacing and calling out, "Shark!"

She squealed, swam to him, and leaped into his arms. "Save me, big strong lifeguard! Save this old damsel in distress!"

He cradled her at the waterline. She seemed weightless as they laughed together. He let her down, and they stood face to face in the water, smiling. She leaned forward and kissed him quickly. "Why, thank you, sir," she said.

Tommy blushed, embarrassed, and felt giddy inside. He avoided looking at her bare breasts, despite being more tempted and anxious to do that than to have a drink. "Well, anytime, my fair lady."

She took his hand, and they went back to the blanket as Whitey waited. They dried off, and he was taken aback by her lack of concern regarding her nudity. She picked up her top, placed it over her breasts, and turned, asking him to tie it off behind her.

They sat down on the blanket, and she sighed deeply. "So, where ya been, stranger? You must be out of food by now. You been cheating on me with one of those chain stores?"

He feigned shock. "My lady Tara. I would never... You're right, though. Whitey and I are down to scraping the inside of cans and eating the grass outside the cabin like goats. We had a trip planned for later today to see you. I've actually been avoiding Mrs. Park, not you," he said, laughing. "I'm doing good."

"Well, I'm glad to hear that," she said.

She understood immediately. That's some intuition, Tommy thought.

"Yeah. I think I'm past it. Just a rough patch, that's all it was. I feel alright now."

He wanted to change the subject away from his weaknesses. "So, this beach is what, clothing optional?"

"Pretty much everything around here is optional. People police themselves. They're hippies, expats, old souls, artists, eclectic types. We're a community of individuals who keep to ourselves, as far as the outside world goes. That can be a very good thing, especially in times like these."

"You're talking about Brand, right?" he asked. "Yeah, I have a real problem with that guy."

"He scares me," Tara said. "I try not to watch much, but I feel conflicted about ignoring it. I worry about the world my future grandchildren will grow up in if that sort of ideology is successful."

"Me too. Someone real close to me is—was—gay. I can't stand to hear the hatred that Brand espouses, not to mention his followers."

She smiled at him. "The strong, sensitive, intelligent type, huh? I love that."

"Well," he stammered. "Not me, though. It's not me, I mean..."

"I didn't think so. It doesn't matter, though. To each his or her own. There's not enough love in the world, Just Tommy."

Her words left him confused about whether she was interested in him or not.

She stood and brushed the sand from herself. "Alright, sir. Time to go and get the stall ready for business."

They picked up their things and walked back to the path together. Tara took his hand and swung it as she sang softly. He didn't know the songs. *I need to brush up on my sixties music.*

They reached the road and paused. Tommy wondered if he should kiss her. He tingled with anticipation, feeling like a nervous kid at a school dance. As he debated, she reached in and gave him a tight hug and kiss on the cheek.

"See you at the market!" she said.

He felt disappointed. *I've never had the balls to be the aggressor—unless I was drunk. Maybe that was part of the problem.* His spirits diminished somewhat as he watched her go down the road in her carefree gait. He was about to turn and go on his way when she twirled around and blew him a kiss.

11 COMPANY

TOMMY CLEANED THE CABIN thoroughly and showered again. A picture now hung over the bullet hole in the wall. He picked out the best clothing he had from the limited selection he'd brought with him in his sea bag. Inspecting himself in the bathroom mirror, he briefly debated whether to shave the beard. *Too risky. Don't get any sloppier than you already have, you fool.*

"Come on, Whitey. Let's head to the market and restock our depleted shelves."

He headed out, with the dog following him. His stamina now improved, he moved at a faster clip than he had on any of their walks so far. *This Forbaxatel is a miracle drug.* He remembered Tara standing in the water, a vision smiling in the sun, and couldn't wait to get to her. The thought of it sent a thrill through him.

They reached the market, and he was disappointed that she wasn't in her stall. It was a little before closing time. He moved past it and walked along the row until he reached Mrs. Park's booth. She sat inside, Buddha-like, eyeing him. He stopped, paused, then walked in.

"You come back for more translation or more rice wine?" she asked. "I think I know." She got up to go to the back, where she had retrieved the last bottle for him.

He wanted to call out to stop her, but something prevented him. He struggled against it as if he were bound too tightly to breathe. *I'm not strong enough yet.* She came back, this time with two bottles wrapped in the same brown paper bags.

"Two for one special, for my best customer. No license. Must buy something else in the store."

He looked around, having given in already.

"You there!" came a voice.

He recognized it immediately. It was the voice of an angel come to rescue him. He turned just in time to embrace her. She was barely there in his arms, so thin and delicate, and she smelled of jasmine.

"Hello, Tara," he said, relieved.

"Come along, stop bothering poor Mrs. Park. I have some things for you back at the stall."

He glanced back at the Korean woman, who was scowling at having lost the sale. *She's the devil on my shoulder, and this one's the angel. That was close.*

Tara took his hand and guided him away. Some of the other vendors wished her good morning, others cat-called and whistled playfully.

When they reached her stall, she invited him to sit. Whitey moved on to lay beside Ol' Jerry.

"Thanks for the rescue," he said, breaking the ice.

"I kind of wanted to stay back and see how the movie was going to end," she said.

"I don't think I would have taken the bottles from her. It was hard, though. I was free of this for so long. I never thought about it. Then I gave up hope on everything else, came here to die.

Damn if that isn't irony—I get a miracle drug, a second lease on life, or more time anyway, and now I have to fight this old battle again."

"Maybe it's not the drug," she said.

"Huh?"

"Maybe you're getting better because you're happy here and in a natural place. Remember what I said before: the body reacts to the spirit in many ways, Just Tommy."

He smiled at her. "I'm ready to believe that. More likely, it's you."

"It's been said that I do have healing properties," she joked.

They talked about life as best they could, Tommy trying to artfully dodge anything related to his past. She didn't seem to want to discuss hers either, and so it worked out well for both of them.

He helped her with the few customers that came by, and soon the stalls around them began packing up for the day.

"I guess I better do my shopping," he said.

She jumped up and retrieved a box from the cooler. "It's done. I have your usual stuff here, and a few other things I want you to try. I went to see Micco and picked up some fish. And if it's alright, I'd like to come by tonight and make dinner for you and Whitey."

The suggestion filled him with joy. "I'm sure you're a far better cook than I am. Invitation accepted. Any time is okay for us, right, Whitey?"

The dog jumped up and bounded onto his lap.

"Micco's off somewhere in his truck. I'd offer you two a ride, but I only have a bicycle," she said. "Unless you want to ride on the handlebars."

"Now that would be something," Tommy said. "We could recreate that scene from *Butch Cassidy and the Sundance Kid*. Remember, when they were playing 'Raindrops Keep Fallin' on My Head?'"

She laughed. "I do remember that. It was an excellent movie, except how it turned out for the vigilantes in the end."

Her use of the word concerned him for a moment. He wondered if she knew more than she was letting on. *If so, she's okay with it, I guess.* "Yeah, that's true. I liked those guys. Anyway, I'm enjoying my daily hikes very much. Whitey and I will see you sometime tonight."

He gave her directions and headed down the road, turning to wave, bow, and blow kisses at several intervals along the way. She responded in kind.

He began to question again whether he was asking for trouble, inviting his own capture. *I came here to keep a low profile; now I'm showing half the damn town where I live and handing out fruit and vegetables to the other half. What the hell is wrong with me? I'm falling in love, that's what.*

He became excited about the chance to spend an evening with her and then terrified as he remembered his physical failure with Carmen. *I'm letting my imagination run wild, getting ahead of myself. She's probably not interested in that. Not with me, anyway.*

~*~

They reached the cabin, and he cleaned up a little, then showered for the third time that day. *Today is like a dream. Maybe I'm in a coma back north or something. Maybe I'm already dead, and this is my heaven.*

He lay down to rest and fell asleep from the exhaustion of the day, with the fresh ocean breeze blowing back the curtains on the window and gliding across his body. He woke to a kiss, and she was there. *It still could be a dream, because she's like a dream...*

"Stay right where you are," she said. "I'm going to start cooking."

His first thought was that wine would be good with dinner. He still craved a drink under any excuse, and he pushed the thought away violently. *I will not let you interfere with this, demon. You can't have me. Not yet, anyway. Maybe at the end.*

She took a break and came to sit next to him, opening her small leather purse and pulling out a joint. "Care for a pre-dinner aperitif?" she asked.

"Don't mind if we do, m'lady," he answered playfully.

Each time they traded it he looked forward to their fingers touching in the exchange. *A small thing can be a mountain when you are new in love.* The evening news had come on, and although he had the television low, Brand's ranting caught her attention.

"Ugh, that guy again," she said. "I don't like to use the word, but I hate him. Everything he stands for. He's just evil. I worry about the world my daughter and future grandchildren will grow up in if he succeeds. I never thought it was possible, and now I'm scared."

Tommy picked up the remote and switched the channel to PBS. "I think we're safe from him on this channel," he said.

"Can you imagine if he actually got elected?" she asked.

"Not much chance," Tommy answered. "Good thing, too. From day one, everything we're proud of and love about this country would start to crumble. He'd do serious damage with judicial appointments, to the environment, to our legacy. He'd turn us all against each other."

Tara frowned. "We'd lose our standing in the world, for sure. We went through this in the sixties, again in the eighties," she said. "Every time I think we're advancing as a society, someone like him, a whole bunch of people with that ideology, come back to try to put us back in the fifties."

Tommy laughed. "The fifties weren't bad if you were a wealthy, white, Christian, heterosexual male. What you said is true, but someone like

FDR always comes along to make America great again. We're resilient."

He was tempted to mention his old and new outlook on life—that he used to tend toward that line of thought: conservative, hateful, racist, homophobic. He was proud of his transformation, but not of his past. He wanted to tell her about his son, how he hadn't accepted Bobby's homosexuality until toward the end of his life. *I didn't know it was almost the end of his life, though.*

He wanted to tell her how proud he was to have changed, and how ashamed he was of his past. He wanted to confess to her, to have her absolve him, to tell him everything would be alright, then for her to love him happily ever after.

She spoke before he could betray himself. "Back then," she said, "in the sixties, I was a campus radical. Against the war and everything about it. I got in with some wrong folks, took it too far. They did some bombings, people got hurt. I'll always have it on my conscience, Tommy. And at some point every day, I wait for them to come and arrest me. You see, Tara isn't my real name, either."

Tommy is my name, he thought. *But not Domingo.* He realized she was crying, and he pulled her close. "We all do things we regret, often when we believe that they're for the greater good. That's what you believed in. You were trying to save lives. Sometimes that costs lives. Sometimes, killing is unavoidable, and the bad have to die to protect the innocent. It's what wars are about and what vigilantes do." *And you're one of us, who would've thought?*

She had confessed to him, and he wanted to confess to her in turn. *Her trail is cold; mine isn't.* He changed the subject before he went too far. She was nestled against him now, curled up on the couch in the fetal position with her head against his chest.

"Were you at Woodstock?" he asked, changing the subject.

"I was," she answered. "Were you in Vietnam?"

"Yes, I was."

"I knew it," they both said at the same time, and they laughed again.

"Everyone should join the Marines," he said. "Teaches discipline."

"Everyone should join the Peace Corps or Greenpeace," she countered. "Teaches respect for others and the planet."

"I wonder why the young people aren't rising up against this Brand guy," he asked. "Like you guys did in the sixties. Don't they realize their world, their future, is at risk of being raped and taken away from them?"

"They're finally starting to," she responded. "They're waking up, and seeing how much this could damage their futures, the very world that they'll grow up in, not to mention their children."

"If it even lasts that long," he said glumly.

"Brighten up, Just Tommy. There's hope. These Republicans know that each generation becomes smarter and more compassionate toward their fellow human beings. And hopefully, less materialistic, status-driven, and greedy. These elections are their last gasp to try to hold it off with legacy tactics, like appointing far-right Supreme Court justices. But society is evolving for the better. It's a kind of metamorphosis. They can't stop that."

She walked over to a small table and picked up a picture on it. She examined it more carefully, then said, "Oh, it's you."

"When I was a younger man, yes. That's my boy, Bobby."

"A couple of big, strong men in the outdoors. I'd love to meet him," she answered.

Tommy was silent. She turned and looked at him, then replaced the picture and took a seat next to him on the couch.

"He's gone, Tara. It's part of the reason I'm here."

"It's okay, Tommy. It's not unusual for people to want to start a new life after a tragedy like that."

That's not the half of it, he thought.

She rubbed his thick white beard. "I love the strong jawline though. You look good without the beard."

"I guess I'm in my Hemingway phase," he said. "Call me Papa. I'm the old man of the sea now. I just hope I don't end like he did."

They ate dinner at the picnic table, treating Whitey to bits underneath. Then they moved back inside and sat on the couch again. He left the TV off.

"I'm sorry I don't have any music," he said.

"I do," she answered. She took her phone out and punched some buttons, and a quiet acoustic rock playlist began. She placed it on the coffee table.

They lay back together wordlessly, and she again took the initiative and put her hand against his cheek, kissing him. They kissed lightly and then more deeply, and she moved to lay atop him. He closed his eyes, determined to burn it all into his memory to replay at the inevitable bad times he knew were somewhere out there in his near future.

They paused for a moment, and he listened to his instincts this time, rising and taking her hand, then scooping her up as she rose and carrying her to the bedroom. He let her down, and she stood before him, slowly removing her simple, long dress. She stood still in the moonlight through the window, braless, down to her underwear. She pushed her panties down over her thighs without breaking their gaze and stepped out of them.

He stood in trembling excitement and terror that his body would let him down, as it had with Carmen; he couldn't move or take his eyes off her. She took one step forward and began to remove his clothes. His shirt first, button by button, from top to bottom, their eyes still locked. When it had dropped to the floor with her dress, she pulled the drawstring on his cotton pants, and they fell almost as if commanded by their owner.

He reached out and cupped the breasts he had been too embarrassed to look at and had longed to touch that day in the clear, warm blue water. Pulling her to him, he felt them against his skin, the buds of her nipples pressed into his chest. He lowered his hands and cupped her buttocks. Drawing her waist against his, he kissed her neck.

She lowered herself to pull off his boxer shorts and take him in her hands. He closed his eyes and touched her soft hair as she began, and he sighed in both ecstasy and relief that his fears were unfounded.

He emptied his mind of everything: every fear, every thought, every bad memory, as they lay down on the small, simple bed and made love in the warm summer air, her light moaning and his heavy breathing mixing with the sounds of the night. The same night that had almost taken him not long ago.

~*~

They lay together as one, her body a perfect fit with his. He caressed her as she lay still, her hand spread out on his chest. He felt like a man again; not a broken man, a sick man, a troubled man. Just a man. They slept until Whitey barked, sensing something out in the darkness.

She roused and checked the clock on his nightstand. "I've got to go, Tommy. The stall never allows a day off."

"It's a shame," he said. "I could stay like this forever."

He got up with her and walked her out. "I'm not comfortable with you going home alone this late. Why don't you stay?"

"I'd love to, but I have to go home and let Ol' Jerry out. His back teeth are probably floating by now. I'm fine; I know this place like the back of my hand. Nothing out there dares to mess with the hippie devil woman of the swamp."

"More like an angel of the night," he said.

She gave him a quick kiss and was off on her bicycle before he could protest again. He watched her go down the road, holding her dress up with one hand, steering crookedly with the other, her hair blowing back in the wind.

12 TRIALS

TARA SHUT OFF THE ALARM CLOCK, exhausted but excited by the events of the night before. She tried to curb herself, remembering the past and her resolve to remain uncommitted and never be hurt again. *I hope he's okay with keeping things casual, and doesn't get all crazy on me.*

She looked out at the dawn and drizzle, relieved that she didn't have to head to the beach for tai chi. She thought about going to him, but didn't want to give the wrong impression. *I just said I wanted to keep it loose, and here I go again. He's so sweet, though. I hope it works out.*

She lay back down on her bed, thinking about her new man, and the tender way he'd made love to her the night before.

She heard her phone ringing and got up reluctantly to answer it.

"Hello, honey," she said, after recognizing the caller ID.

"Hi, Mom. I'm just checking in from up here in the cold North. I miss you."

"I miss you too, baby. How's school going? Do you like New York?"

"New York, not so much, but school is good. I have great profs, so I'm enjoying classes. I'm also doing a lot of campus activism against the Brand campaign."

"Glad to hear it, my sweet girl. The rest of the country doesn't know him like we former West Virginians do. We need to get the word out. The man's a cancer on humanity and the planet."

"I'm trying my best. Hey, I saw on the news that there's some crazy vigilante guy from up here on the loose. They suspect he's somewhere down there in Florida. He killed a priest and a cop or something like that."

Tara laughed. "Well, I haven't seen any vigilante-killer types yet. Same thing as always—retirees and eclectic loners. Florida is a pretty big place. He's probably all the way down to Key

West by now, working on getting across to Havana."

"Okay, Mom. Be careful anyway. You're too trusting—always trying to find the good in everyone, no matter how little there is to work with. You always took people in like stray dogs. Stray dogs too, come to think of it."

~*~

Tommy rose early and fretted over whether he should go to tai chi, if that would be too aggressive, or if she'd get the wrong idea if he didn't. *Love is confusing.* As the darkness outside faded, he realized it was drizzling, and the decision was made for him. "I guess that settles that, Whitey."

He went to the couch and sat back, closing his eyes, pretending she was still there against him. He forced his imagination to smell her, touch her, hear her, feel her. When that wasn't enough, he went to the bedroom and stood, eyes closed again, and replayed the scene. He felt himself becoming aroused without stimulation, something that hadn't happened in a long time.

Breaking the spell, he went to the window again and looked down the long path leading to his cabin, hoping to see her. Whitey stared at him expectantly, and Tommy let him out to relieve himself.

Brand was on the morning news. It was a clip from a press conference the previous night. He was attesting again to his love of the military and law enforcement. *Draft-dodger and crooked businessman, breaking laws every day. Hypocrite.* He turned off the set, pushing the negativity of Brand away.

He couldn't remember being this happy or falling in love this quickly before. He allowed his mind to play its tricks: imagining that the drug's effects were permanent, that the two gruesome murders that he'd been a part of hadn't happened, that he was here after a divorce, and would live many years happily growing old in this quiet, tranquil paradise with the woman of his dreams.

The thought reminded him that he hadn't taken his pills. He went to the kitchen and took the herbals that he had bought at the Asian apothecary with Sensei Molletier. He pulled the bottle of Forbaxatel from the shelf, taking note of its lightness and rattling sound. Opening it, he saw four remaining pills. *Shit. One bottle left.* He washed the pill down and went to the bedroom to retrieve the last large bottle of the pills.

I'm going to have to figure out how to get more of this. Maybe get back into the trial under my new identity; it's worth a shot if it's the only one I have. Feeling around in the space beneath, Tommy moved aside the stacks of bills, the firearm, ammunition, and few remaining valuables. Not feeling the bottle of pills, he pulled the items out and searched the space. Still coming up empty, he grabbed his flashlight and used it to peer in all the corners. *Nothing. Must've left them in the sea bag.*

He pulled his sea bag from the closet and stuck his arm in up to his shoulder, moving items around, searching for the pill bottle. Starting to panic, he yearned to hear its rattle. He began pulling items from the bag and then moving faster, dumping the contents onto the floor. He dropped to his knees, scrambling across the floor to check every item that had fallen.

He ran back to the kitchen, opening drawers, flinging the contents to the floor. It didn't take him long to toss the small house thoroughly, and finally, he threw himself on the bed, accepting the realization that had crept into his mind not long before. *I insisted that Molletier take them, even though he continually refused. I said I didn't really want to live all that long, just buy some time in paradise and die somewhere nice.*

Everything that had been giving him joy a moment ago fell away in an instant. He noticed the two small black vials among the mess strewn across the floor.

~*~

Tara plopped down in front of her laptop computer and stared at the screen-saver. It was a picture of her and Tim in ski gear, smiling with rosy cheeks and ice-frosted eyelashes. *Cheater. Liar. I guess it's time I finally change my settings.* She logged in and went through her gallery of pictures, trying to find another to replace it. *I need a picture of Tommy and me.*

Only in viewing the gallery of thumbnails did she realize how unlucky in love she had really been. She had given her heart to each of them and been promised the same in return, only to be let down in the end. *Thus, I find myself here, in paradise. Alone.*

She thought back to the morning on the beach. *Just Tommy. He seems kind of nice. Fun. Not too full of himself. Not overly aggressive. He was cute and shy, not wanting to look at me. So different from the others. He sure passed that test.*

She thought about what Tommy had said about his illness and the miracle cure. *Doesn't make sense. What was the trial he mentioned? Forbaxatel? Let's see...*

She opened a browser and visited a few of the sites she remembered from her nursing days. None of them yielded information on the drug. She did an internet search, which resulted in some hits. She read through the uses, dosage, side effects, interactions, and comments on the trial results.

"Called the anti-chemo for its temporary rejuvenating effects." *Temporary.*

"Should only be used under the supervision of a physician." *Something's not right.*

"When the cancer has developed a resistance to this drug, it comes back aggressively, and life expectancy is significantly reduced, perhaps less than it would have been under standard treatment." *Oh, Tommy. This isn't good.*

"Because of these problems, the trial has been suspended."

Tara stopped to try to make sense of it all. She wondered how he could be taking a discontinued experimental drug in the middle of nowhere, without a doctor's supervision. *Is he a doctor, perhaps? Was he on the trial and didn't return his supply of the drug? Maybe he bought it on the black market.*

She liked him and wanted to believe the best, as she always did. She thought about the pictures in her gallery. *As I always have.*

She went back to the search results, scrolling down to look for more information. One toward the bottom of the list caught her eye. "New York Man Still Wanted in Cop Murder and Trial Drug Heist."

She hesitated, then clicked the link. The picture stared back at her. It wasn't the kind man with the white Hemingway beard, but it was clearly the one she had seen in the picture in his living room—the clean-cut version of the very same person. When she recovered from her initial shock and found the courage, she continued reading the article.

13 WANTED MAN

TOMMY SAT ON HIS COUCH with the television on, staring past it and out of the window to the brightly lit day. On the coffee table in front of him lay a notebook, a pen, a black vial, and a loaded 9mm handgun with the safety off. Whitey lay next to him, sleeping.

He looked over at the dog. *I never did ask Tara about taking care of you, because everything got better. You're better off without me, Whitey. You and Tara both. Now I don't have long. I want to go out like this, healthy and happy, not decrepit, miserable, and a burden on her. Business first.*

He picked up the notebook and began writing his last letters. He struggled to write the first one through the tears that fell. The second was easier. Then he started the third letter.

Dearest Tara,

Whitey suddenly jumped up and ran to the door, startling Tommy. He rose quickly to look down the path out front and saw her coming, moving fast on her bicycle. He ran back to the living room, scurrying to put everything away. He had just finished and flopped back down on the couch when she rushed through the door.

"We have to talk," she said.

"Yes, we do," Tommy answered. "Please sit down."

She did, and they locked eyes. "You've been crying," she said.

"Not a tough guy like me." He motioned to the kitchen. "Damn onions."

"Tommy, I told you I was a nurse. I wanted to help you. I was trying to do some research on the drug you're taking. I was worried that you didn't seem to have a physician in the loop."

"Yeah, about that..." he started to say.

"Wait. I don't think you know what you're doing. Forbaxatel was discontinued. As you know, it had miraculous, rejuvenating results early in the trial." She took his hand.

"I know, that's why I..."

"But then, Tommy..." She had started to cry, and the words were not coming easily. "But then, when the trial stops or the cancer figures it out, it comes back hard. With a vengeance."

Tommy hung his head. "Just my luck. Vigilante cancer, how ironic."

Her tone changed, anger creeping in. "Which leads me to the other thing. When I was searching for the drug, I saw a story. A news article about a fugitive wanted for his involvement in two murders. Actually, two fugitives, who stole a lot of Forbaxatel from a hospital pharmacy. One of them is still on the run. Allegedly, somewhere in Florida. Tommy Borata."

He looked at her, trying to decide what to say.

"I didn't lie to you, Tara. I did retire. I just didn't tell you everything. How could I? And I never dreamed we would get involved. Well, maybe I did dream, but I never thought it was possible. I wanted to keep a low profile. Then I fell in love with you. After that, I wanted to protect you. It's called plausible deniability. I figured we'd ride it out together down here. Everything changed when I started getting better."

"You were involved in two deaths, Tommy. How could you..."

"And you indicated you may have been as well. We're not all that different, Tara."

She reacted swiftly, slapping him hard. "Don't you dare compare anything I've done to those gruesome murders..."

He became angry. "Dead is dead. If people died, what difference does that make? I know all about you sixties radicals and the bombings. That's no delicate way to die. We talked about this. Bad people need to die sometimes, so that good people don't die."

He hesitated and then softened his tone. "That priest molested a lot of kids, including my boy. That cop made my son's life miserable, taunting and bullying him relentlessly until I was sure he was going to kill himself. Then he killed my Bobby. He killed my beautiful boy, Tara."

Tommy paused as emotion overcame him, then took a deep breath and continued. "The cop was as crooked as they come, and he was hell bent on locking me up. I was just trying to clean the world up on the way out, to make up for who I used to be and mistakes I made. Me, Moses, and Sensei Molletier—that's what we were all dedicated to."

She looked at him, weeping. "I don't know what to do. Everything was so different just a day ago. I have feelings for you, Tommy. But what you did..."

"Listen," he interrupted her. "You have options. You can turn me in, or you can pretend you never saw that article. Hopefully, they don't figure out that you searched on that trial drug and put two and two together and come looking for us here. That's the new kind of investigation my kid did with the police force."

He realized he was scaring her, and calmed down a bit. "I'm almost out of the drug, and I'm out of time, Tara. I don't want to ruin your life as well. Take a day to think about it. It's a big decision. We both need time to think, and we both have decisions to make."

Their discussion had relegated the television to background noise, but in the silence that followed his last comment, the morning newscast came to the foreground, and they watched.

"With the shocking results last night from five state primaries, Candidate Brand has won the Republican nomination for President of the United States."

They looked at each other in disbelief. "He's going to win this thing," Tommy said in quiet acceptance. "This son of a bitch is going to win and take this whole goddamn country down."

"I don't think so, Tommy. It's a protest vote against the Republicans. The people won't allow him to win the presidency."

"Have you seen the crowds? It's a movement. The 'protest' is massive. I think he's going to do it. It won't matter for me, but it will for people I love. Like you, and your kid."

The news brought a further decline in their mood.

"Wait," Tommy said suddenly. "You said *one of them* is still on the run. Did the article talk about the sensei? He's locked up? Is he in South Korea, or did they extradite him?"

She retook his hand. "He never made it, Tommy. They were waiting for him by the time he went to the airport to fly out. He backed off and holed up in New Jersey. He was doing okay, concealing his identity and laying low, until he ran out of the pills and started to go downhill. By the time they found him and closed in, he was in pretty bad shape."

"Oh no," Tommy said.

She continued. "The cancer didn't get him. He got a tip that they were coming. He'd been following it on the news. They found him in his bed. He had taken some kind of poison. It said he had left a note for you."

"Doesn't matter," Tommy said. "I'll see him soon. Moses too."

"How many of the pills do you have left, Tommy?"

"Four."

"Oh my God," she said. "We can stretch them out. I know how."

"And what?" he replied. "I get a few extra days out of it before I start going downhill fast?"

"Every day is a gift, Just Tommy. If I can get even a few extra days with you, I'll take them. Why don't we forget everything and spend them together? I know of a place right on the water not far from here that we can use. It's remote, all by itself on a small key. Friends of mine own it but rarely use it. I'll get Micco's brother to run the stall for me for a while. He likes the extra money. We'll have a little vacation, just you and me. You'll start to get sick after that, but I'll take care of you. I know how to do that, too. I love you, Just Tommy."

"I love you, Tara. I don't want to be selfish. I don't deserve you. The cops might find me before the cancer takes me out. It might bring attention to you, and that would be bad. I would be a tortured soul in the hereafter, knowing I came into yet another beautiful life and ruined it. You could go to jail."

"I'll take that risk. Besides, I know nothing. Some crazy Hemingway-looking retired guy came here and stole my heart. That's all I know."

"I need to know something. Will you take care of Whitey for me?"

"Of course, any time you need it. I love Whitey too."

"I mean…forever. After I'm gone."

"Of course, Tommy." She kissed him, and the stress and pain went away from him for as long as their lips touched.

She disengaged and looked him in the eyes. "Anyway, sound like a plan, mister?"

"It sounds good to me. Go take care of business, Tara. Let's take the day to think things over, and get together tonight to talk more. We've been hit with a lot today. I want to make sure you aren't just acting out of the emotion and shock of the moment."

They embraced outside the bungalow, and she left on her bicycle, singing as she went down the path to the road.

Tommy returned to the cabin. He was saddened and overwhelmed by the news of the Sensei's passing and Brand's nomination. He turned the television back on and sat down on the couch. *I have decisions to make. Big ones.*

He thought about the letters he'd been writing and the gun and black vial that were hastily stashed in his bedroom dresser. He weighed his earlier inclination to end it all against spending his remaining time with Tara. *Killing myself isn't fair to her. It's not heroic. It's not how I want to go out.*

The news was showing exclusive coverage. Brand was preening before a large audience. Tommy paused to listen.

"I'll return the country to a place of God; I'll turn back the perversion that is overtaking us because we allow those gay heathens free rein and equality with normal people. I'll unshackle our police to use their full force on the scum that fills our cities. I'll return our country to a military powerhouse and destroy our enemies."

Brand paused at the mic for dramatic effect, and the crowd grew quiet in anticipation. "In closing, I want to announce that we'll kick off our presidential campaign with an extraordinary event. To honor our brave, heroic military veterans, I will hold a special rally and event in Miami very soon."

At that moment, Tommy felt a renewed purpose.

14 TEMPORARY UTOPIA

EACH OF THE FOLLOWING DAYS was the same: discrete, singular, and perfect. Each was a thing unto itself—packaged and treasured like the remaining pills that kept him whole.

As they rose every morning to enjoy the sunrise, they renewed their vow to live in the moment; to not anticipate the hours ahead and to not dread having used each one up.

Tara always woke first and watched him sleep until he began to stir. She gazed at him, wondering what dreams a man might have, knowing his time on earth was so short. At times he seemed blissful, and she hoped he was dreaming of her. Other times he wore a mask of consternation and thrashed in his sleep as if trying to break free from unseen bonds.

She allowed herself to wonder what life would've been like had she met him earlier; before everything had come to this. He seemed to be the one she'd always hoped would come into her life.

When he finally began to wake each day, she would put her hands on him, massaging muscles that had been ravaged and wasted by the disease. Some days, the massage made way to making love, but other times they just held each other until finally giving in to the rays of sun that rose over the ocean to invade the room.

They began each morning with tai chi, meditation, and a light breakfast on the beach, and she could see that it was bringing him peace. They spent the bulk of every day there, under a large umbrella on the ratty green wool military-issue blanket. They each chose a book from the well-stocked bookshelf in the cabin and read passages aloud dramatically, laughing at each other's lack of theatrical skill.

When they became too warm, they rose and went to the water, shedding their clothing to the sand along the way. They swam far out, rising and falling together in the rolling waves, and playfully chased each other and held each other, laughing, each time the prize had been captured.

At times he would rise up and walk off on his own, often stopping to gaze out over the endless ocean, and she watched from the blanket. He would return and sit quietly, and she knew not to disturb him until he came around to her.

Their meals were light, simple, and organic. Tara had chosen the best items from her stall and the market's other vendors and stocked the kitchen well.

As each late afternoon began to give way to evening, they returned to the cabin to clean up, then went back to the beach for the sunset. They refused the television and took their dinner each evening by candlelight. Some nights they played board games, laughing at each other's clumsy and blatant attempts to cheat.

They retired each night to the sparse paneled bedroom, disrobing to sleep naked as they had agreed, and made love slowly and passionately as the evening breeze billowed the curtains into the room, carrying the scent of the ocean and the sound of the waves from outside, which seemed to crash in time. And then they would lie in the dark, holding each other until they fell asleep.

They smoked pot, but not to excess, finding their times of clarity more enjoyable.

One evening, after they had eaten dinner and were waiting on the beach for the sunset, she produced a Thermos.

"Would you like to try something?" she asked.

"Coffee? Sure."

"No, something very different. This is peyote tea. Micco makes it. Natives in the Southwest have used it for hundreds of years for ceremonies, medicine, and visions. Especially for healing ceremonies, so hey, you never know!"

"What the hell," Tommy said. "I got nothing to lose. Let's give it a try and have a little ceremony right here on the beach."

"Fair warning, Tommy. It's a psychedelic; it contains mescaline. You'll be tripping. One of the rules the natives had was that no negativity could be introduced. Everything had to be positive. I'll be your spiritual guide."

"How could anything be negative, here on this beach with someone like you?" he asked.

She removed the plastic cup from the top of the Thermos and poured some for him. He took a sip and gagged.

"Good lord, this is horrible," he said.

"Yeah, it's best to just toss it down the hatch," she laughed.

He did so, and then she poured a cup for herself and consumed it.

"Can you imagine, Tara," he asked, "if every day of life was like this? Maybe in some advanced version of society, when robots are doing everything for us?"

"It already is, Tommy, for people like me and the others who live here. They have to sacrifice material things, but they do it, so they don't donate their lives to running on a hamster wheel to make others wealthy."

"I wish someone would've told me that a long time ago," he said wistfully. "This is the kind of life my son Bobby would have flourished in."

They laid back down, looking up at the stars that were appearing as dusk gave way to a clear night. They pointed out constellations to each other while waiting.

~*~

Tommy was about to tell her that it wasn't affecting him. Then he looked up at the stars and sensed a tingling, like a mild electric current, but not just physical—he sensed it in his spirit, in his psyche, as well.

"I think it's hitting me," he said.

She took his hand. "Go with the flow. Go easy, be one with the universe."

As he lay there, he seemed to become more attuned to everything in the environment. He heard the rush of waves and felt he could sense their building and crashing, and then their return to the ocean. He felt the creatures of the sea, not far away: the gentle whales and dolphins, the fearsome sharks, the graceful, beautiful manta rays.

The stars above seemed to realign and signal to him. He saw patterns in them, and the patterns changed. He felt a symbiotic connection to everything at once: the earth, space beyond, nature, and...something else. Something he couldn't quite perceive, but it was there, at the edge of his grasp.

She seemed to know, without him having to say a word. "Don't think too hard," she said. "Let it come to you. Relax, observe, perceive."

He closed his eyes and felt a light floating sensation, then something like sleep, but not sleep. "It's beautiful, Tara. It's so beautiful."

He did as she said, and then it was there-the edge of a dimension that was imperceptible to the normal mind. *Maybe it's heaven.* He closed his eyes and tried not to push, but to move into it. Everything grew silent, and he felt transported to another spiritual plane.

"Well, if it ain't my favorite cracker," he heard Moses say in his unmistakable deep baritone. The words didn't come through his ears—they were simply in his mind.

Moses, oh, Moses. I'm so sorry.

"Nothin' to be sorry about, Tommy."

Are you in heaven? Is there a God?

"There ain't no heaven or hell, but there is good and bad. The spirit is perpetual, and your physical form is just a vessel, my brother. It's a cycle, repeated until the spirit is cleansed and ready for eternity.

"The one you seek, he's of the bad. Some are unredeemable, Tommy, doomed to the cycle in eternity. Remember what your Good Book says—'In his place shall arise a contemptible person to whom royal majesty has not been given. He shall come in without warning and obtain the kingdom by flatteries.'"

Brand. Screw him, Mos. Where's my boy, Bobby? Is he there? Can I talk to him?

"He's here, Tommy. We're all here, and we'll see you soon. You have found the goodness within you."

What about the sensei? Is he okay?

He waited, and there was silence. He became aware of his body again, Tara's hand in his. He opened his eyes and looked back up at the stars, and once again heard the symphony of the waves.

"Are you okay?" she asked.

"Yeah. I just had some kind of...out-of-body experience, I guess you would call it."

"I'm glad you're back," she said.

They sat up and looked over the ocean discussing the fragility of life and what might come after. He didn't want to talk about what he'd experienced. He was afraid she'd question his sanity.

"You know what, Tara? I think that this human form is only the beginning of our spiritual life. Our bodies and minds in this state are in their crudest form, embryonic during our whole time here, and when we pass from this life, we metamorphose into something much better in the next stage. Unless we're not ready; then we come back, to learn more, to evolve our spirit further."

"It makes sense to me, Just Tommy. Reincarnation is one of the oldest theories in faith. Maybe the ancients knew a lot more than we give them credit for. We dismiss their beliefs as superstition too quickly."

"I wonder," Tommy replied, "if we only stay alive sometimes because we're so afraid, not knowing what comes after. Maybe if we did, we wouldn't mind dying so much when our time comes nearer."

They talked until the sun came up. They spoke of the life they could have had together, vowing to find each other in whatever came after it and to spend their eternity together with days exactly like the ones they'd been enjoying. She removed a delicate silver necklace with a peace-sign medallion from her neck and placed it around his. "I want you to have it," she said. "It's a part of me."

The remaining days and nights passed slowly.

"It's funny," he said one evening, as they were both beginning to drift into sleep. "I'm at the end of the road, this long, hard tortured life, and I've never been happier. Never been more at peace. It took this long."

"Well then, I've accomplished my goal," she said.

Their stay came to its end on the day after he took his last dose of the medicine, and they silently packed to leave.

~*~

On the second morning after they returned, Tara rode her bicycle to the market to open up for the day. She hadn't heard from Tommy, and had patiently given him his space. She decided she would go to his bungalow after she closed for the day if he hadn't turned up by then.

As she removed the lock and pulled up the rolled canvas fronting, Whitey came bounding out, startling her. Her shock and surprise at seeing the dog turned to happiness almost immediately.

"Whitey! Come here, you little bundle of joy." She picked up the excited dog and peered inside the still-dark stall. She crept in cautiously, carrying Whitey, who was wriggling in her arms.

She loved Tommy's playful games. "Okay, mister. I know you're in here somewhere." She peered behind the displays of seed packets, excited at the game, eager with anticipation. "Just Tommy, Just Tommy, ready or not here I come…"

She made her way around the displays of silent fruit and vegetables, looking beneath them. "You're making me work way too hard, good sir. Come, and present yourself to your lady in waiting."

The plywood door to the small back office area caught her eye. "Ah, taking over my enterprise, I see. I've got you cornered now, buddy."

She smiled as she pulled it open, and the dog looked at her sadly.

The desk lamp over her small hutch was on, and a white envelope lay on her closed laptop. Written on it, in small letters, was "Tara."

15 MEN AT SEA

TOMMY WALKED THE DOCKS, shining his flashlight on the back of each boat he approached. Despite his sadness, he was at peace. The lapping of the waves against their hulls seemed to encourage him, to lead him on to his destiny.

The sea bag chafed at his shoulder, and he paused to shift it to the other side. The decrepit fishing vessels in the darkened area contrasted sharply against the sleek white pleasure yachts in the adjacent marina, which was lit by the glare of overhead floodlights.

As he neared the end of the pier, the boats seemed to become older and shabbier. He pointed the flashlight beam at the stern of the very last one and saw what he'd been searching for—

April. He tossed the sea bag in and stepped over the gunwale.

Noticing a dim light in the cabin, he made his way toward the steps. The door swung open, and Micco waved.

"Seas are relatively calm," Micco said. "It'll take several hours to get up to Miami. Get comfortable. There's water in the cooler and a Thermos of coffee up here in the pilothouse if you want to hang out with me."

"Coffee sounds good," Tommy responded, climbing up into the cabin. "Thanks again, Micco."

"Thank you, Tommy. What you're paying me for this charter would cover a week's profit at the fish stall. I'll have you there well before sunrise, like you wanted."

"But you'll keep it between us, right? If you get pushed on it, just say you chartered your boat to an old Marine sailor who was dying and wanted one last voyage to see his family."

"Got it." Micco began to navigate the boat through the narrow canals to sea. "I don't know what you're up to, so essentially, that's accurate."

Tommy surveyed the cabin. Behind the two captain's chairs was a small cot, and a counter and sink for cleaning fish. The boat had apparently seen better days; many of the fixtures and equipment had been patched or repaired with zip ties and duct tape. The engine strained and rattled, even at the low speed they were traveling.

"You, ah, ever taken it this far away?" Tommy asked.

"No, just my usual local fishing circuit off the coast."

Tommy frowned and decided not to worry. He was on a mission; in the hands of fate with nothing to lose and little time left. Still, his heart ached for the woman he'd left behind. He missed Whitey, his constant companion, and worried that the dog would be upset at being left behind.

"You mind if I catch some sleep?" Tommy asked.

"Go for it," Micco responded.

He moved to the small cot and lay on his back, thinking through his plan again and again. Searching for any holes, putting contingencies in place for anything that could fail. The smell of diesel fuel filled his nostrils, and he found himself flashing back to the amphibious vehicles he had been in off the coast of Vietnam, so long ago.

~*~

He had just arrived in-country, green from training, full of piss and vinegar, and now that he was there, he was scared out of his mind.

The M113A1 Green Dragon Armored Personnel Carrier he was in was cramped, and the other ten men sitting below in benches against its walls spewed bravado. The vehicle was on reconnaissance, rambling through the jungle as they laughed and joked in its belly.

There was a sudden acceleration, and the commander in the turret was heard shouting. Their .50 caliber Browning M2 machine gun began rattling off rounds. The bursts stopped, and the leader's limp body was passed down from the hatch as the vehicle swerved out of control.

The medic immediately jumped up to provide first aid to the wounded man, as one of the top gunners took control of the vehicle and shouted that they were pinned down and going to attempt to cross the river to escape. Tommy was frozen in place, eighteen years old and wondering if he was in a bad dream or war movie. He wanted to be home, in his bedroom, safe.

They began to hear the unmistakable sound of machine-gun rounds hitting the vehicle. Some pierced the light armor, and daylight showed through randomly appearing holes in its walls. They all hunched down, and he heard a splash as the vehicle entered the water. He remembered that the vehicle was "moderately amphibious" and looked around at the men weighed down with battle armor and weapons.

He checked his M14 rifle nervously. They bobbed in the water, and he could feel the rush of the river taking the craft under its own control. He was convinced at that point that he was going to die there, in that aluminum tin can full of sweaty, smelly men.

"Do not panic, you are United States Marines!" Sergeant Campbell shouted at them. "Keep your composure! We are not going to die here today, Marines!" He looked at the other men, who all wore grim determination on their faces. Tommy hoped he didn't look as scared as he was.

The carrier swayed and bounced, and he heard the water sloshing against the hull, thinking that if it sank without deploying its hatch, they would all have to somehow exit through the turret above. They were all thrown to the floor as the vehicle slammed into an obstacle in the water and stopped. The hatch deployed, and he heard Campbell yell, "Cover yourselves, exit, *now!*"

They got up and charged the rectangular doorway, weapons held high above their heads to try and keep them dry. The vision of the men in front of him struggling in the current, trying to stay on their feet, rounds dancing off the water, was forever burned into his mind. He was last, except for the sergeant, who shoved him out. "Go, Borata, damn it!"

He remembered the welcome chill of the water and fresh air, after being cramped in the sweaty compartment breathing diesel fumes for so long. He saw a man ahead of him go limp, and the river took him away, streams of blood trailing behind him in the water. His adrenaline surged further.

And then he stumbled and fell. He opened his eyes and saw only green-brown water rushing around him. He remembered wondering how long he could hold his breath, and if he could somehow remove all of his heavy gear. *No chance,* he remembered thinking. *I'm going to die here today.*

And then he felt himself being dragged up by the collar. As the water washed from his eyes, he saw Campbell, the toughest man he had ever known, in his face.

"Keep going, damn it, or you'll get us both killed, Borata!"

He regained his feet and pushed through the water, Campbell continually urging him on from behind. And then he didn't hear him anymore. They were almost to the shoreline. He turned and saw Campbell lying across a large root, hanging onto it, blood mixing with the wet fatigues around his chest.

Tommy turned back toward him.

"No, you idiot, go back!" Campbell said, barely audible over the din. "That's a fucking order, Lance Corporal!"

Tommy continued to push against the current to him, having lost his weapon already. He heard round after round of gunshots, and hoped the Marines on the shore were covering him.

Reaching Campbell, he dragged him off the branch and towed him across the remaining stretch of river with every ounce of energy the adrenaline provided him. He remembered his heart pounding in his ears, all of the other sounds disappearing.

The last thing he remembered was being hit in the leg and collapsing at the waterline, pulling Campbell up alongside him and out of the water. The sergeant was unconscious, but still breathing.

~*~

He dozed off, and sometime later the transition from the loud, erratic churning of the diesel engine to silence caused him to wake. The boat wasn't moving, and Micco wasn't in the captain's chair. He heard cursing and banging, and rose to find Micco in the stern with the engine compartment open.

"What the hell?" Tommy asked. "I thought you said this tub could make it?"

"No," Micco replied. "I only said I haven't taken it this far."

Tommy hopped up and joined him. They worked together to diagnose the problem, going through a litany of troubleshooting steps by flashlight. Tommy located and pulled the fuel filter, shining his light on it. The paper folds were covered in gunk. "Christ, Micco. What kind of shit fuel are you putting in this thing, and when's the last time you changed this filter?"

"I'm a fisherman, not a mechanic. I have a guy that does all that for me."

"I guess you don't have a spare on board."

"Of course not."

"Alright. We can run without it the rest of the way, but you'll have to get it replaced in Miami. Get me some waterproof tape to splice this fuel line."

Micco rummaged in his toolbox as Tommy began the repair.

"Tommy, we have company. Get below, quick."

Tommy lifted his head slightly above the gunwale and saw a Coast Guard cutter approaching. He hit the floor, grabbed his sea bag, and crawled to the staircase. He sailed down the stairs head-first to the marine head and shut the door behind him, panting to catch his breath.

He listened as the cutter pulled alongside, and felt the boat rock as they boarded. They started asking Micco questions about where he was going, what he was doing in this part of the ocean in this type of vessel. Each of their heavy footsteps above caused Tommy's heart to pound harder and faster. He heard Micco start to explain that he had a buyer in Miami for the craft. *Good thinking, kid.*

The discussion went on, and he heard them ask Micco for papers for himself and the boat. The small, cramped toilet seemed to close in on him. He was sweating profusely, and the stench of the head and rocking of the ship was causing his nausea and panic to build. He started to wonder if the disease was contributing to the way he felt. Reaching under his shirt, he began to press around his liver, stomach, and kidneys.

He resisted the urge to bolt from the compartment so that he could breathe fresh air. He thought about Tara, back there somewhere, and wondered if she was thinking about him. He hoped she wasn't angry. He thought about the small white dog, and the pain in his heart began to match his physical discomfort.

For a moment he considered retrieving the 9mm from his sea bag. *No. I can't kill them; they're innocent.* He thought about holding them captive, but then he'd have to draw Micco into this. *He doesn't deserve that either. That scenario would get very messy. As it would if I used the gun on myself...*

He fished around in a pocket and withdrew a small black vial. He held it and considered opening it and downing the contents. *I'm screwed. Let's just get this over with.*

He then worried that Micco would be suspected of killing him, and decided to wait to see how things would play out above. He tightened his grip on the cap, deciding he would twist it off at the first sign that they were about to breach his hiding place.

16 FAN MAIL

BRENDA SAT AT HER DESK, passing the time by opening a large stack of mail for Brand. It was the usual mix of crackpots, haters, and devotees. Some letters went directly into the trash; others went into a pile designated for form-letter responses, campaign items, and signed photographs. None ever went to Brand himself; he couldn't be bothered.

The return address on one caught her attention. She opened it, hopeful it would be a good candidate. Brand wanted a stage full of adoring veterans to accompany him, but due to his rhetoric many of the people they'd contacted had declined the offer.

"This guy looks good," she said to Stinson. "Bronze Star with a V for Valor and Purple Heart in Vietnam. Disabled. Big fan."

"What's the name?" Stinson asked. "I'll add him to the list and verify his background."

"Thomas Robert Domingo," she answered. "I want this guy. Start the process, and I'll reach out to him." She noticed that he had left no phone info, only a P.O. box in Miami. She opened her laptop to get a letter ready to send out. "He's local too, bonus."

She began to feel bad, and couldn't quite put her finger on why. She stopped what she was doing and walked over to the window to look looked down at the people moving about in the city. The nattily dressed professionals, middle-class office workers, and blue-collar workers, all seemed to be hurried, stressed. They were too far below for her to make out their faces, but she could tell from their body postures that they weren't smiling or happy. *They're stressed the fuck out. I know, because I'm one of them.*

"How do you think it happened, Stinson?"

He looked up from his laptop. "What?"

"If I think about the fifties, sixties, even seventies, if people worked hard, they could have a comfortable life. They could afford a house, vacations, a functional car, and a pension to retire comfortably. Actually, even if it was just one of them working, nine-to-five. They had nights and weekends to spend together, to raise their kids."

"That's how it was for my parents. I remember it," Stinson replied.

Brenda shook her head. "Now, both spouses have to work their asses off, and it seems they *still* aren't getting any of those things. Why?" She turned and looked at Stinson for his response.

"The answer's easy," he said. He pointed at the oversized portrait of Brand. "Because of people like that. In the past, when the economy was good, workers' wages followed suit, in lock-step. Look at the graphs on the internet. Executive compensation always mirrored raises and bonuses for everyone all the way down the line back then.

"The eighties brought the era of extreme greed. Reagan's trickle-down economics plan was an endorsement of greed. That's when you see the curves start moving away from each other—theirs goes up, ours goes down. People like him," he gestured at Brand's portrait again, becoming angry, "started hoarding more and more of it for themselves. They're taking society down with their greed, at least every tier below themselves.

"But they don't care, because they'll be set for generations. Look at the results, as people no longer have time or energy to parent their kids. They come home late, worn out emotionally and physically, and just don't have the patience. They aren't there to prevent bad decisions. We end up with a lot of screwed-up kids who become screwed-up adults."

"So," she said, "you hate him too. I've always been afraid to ask."

"I'm not even sure hate's a strong enough word. I've wanted to quit since day one. I just wanted this on my resume. I figured we'd lose quick, and that would be that. Now it's like I'm on this terrifying amusement-park ride and no matter how much I cry or scream to get off, nobody can hear me, I just have to wait until it ends on its own."

"Exactly," she said. "Well, we're almost at the end of the ride, I guess. People will figure him out now that he's got the spotlight almost to himself. They'll see that he's a fraud: in debt, a pathological liar who hates the people in his base. He's a narcissistic, corrupt, unintelligent, lazy, and a drunk. They'll see that now, right? Won't the Democrats massacre him on all of that?"

"I always thought he had a snowball's chance in hell—that he'd need a perfect storm. And that's what he's gotten so far. It's what scares the hell out of me. Not so much that I'll have to stay on the terrifying ride even longer, but now the rest of the world might be coming along, for at least four more years. If the planet lasts that long under his reign of terror."

Brenda felt her discomfort grow. "You're scaring the hell out of me now, Stinson. I'm wondering if he's got our offices bugged. That'll be the end of us."

"And you're complaining? I'm kind of hoping." They both laughed at the thought.

"Well," Stinson continued. "We've got our big-time political experience now. Everyone knows our names."

"That's the problem. We'll never find work again. We'll be almost as hated as Brand is. I guess we'll just have to continue to hitch our wagons to him."

"Think again, Brenda. What have we seen of him? He demands loyalty from everyone, but never gives it. As soon as he's done with people, he throws them aside like a half-finished sandwich that he's grown bored with."

"Well, if he does ever make it somehow, there'd be hell to pay. Not only is it impossible to deliver the things he's promised, but he also has no intention of doing it."

"Doesn't matter," Stinson said. "Once he's in, he won't give a shit about any of that. He'll just focus on being king. Everyone said he had no chance because he's inexperienced. But he's a born, natural bullshit artist. It's in his DNA, and he's been practicing all his life.

"He'll continue to bullshit his way out of every situation while he works on breaking down the system enough to lock himself in forever. Like every other dictator in history has done. Our mistake has been in believing it could never happen here."

"Unless someone shoots him," Brenda said, laughing. "That's why I try not to stand next to him."

"Don't ever say that Brenda," Stinson said. "Don't ever say it."

17 NATIVE HERITAGE

TOMMY HEARD one of the Coast Guardsmen inquire about the open engine hatch, and then Micco explaining about the fuel filter. He asked them if they had any waterproof tape to spare. Tommy felt the boat rock as one of them went back to his craft to retrieve it.

The other guardsman's footsteps approached the stairway leading to his location. He heard him ask if he could use the head. *Don't come in here, Coastie. There's a fucking desperate Marine in here.*

"Sure, go ahead," Micco said.

Micco—What? Tommy felt panic at the words and gripped the vial in both hands. *I'll explain to them quickly that I hijacked him, then down this.*

"Fair warning, though," Micco continued, "it's been clogged up for days, and I haven't been able to dump it. Hold your nose if you're going down there." *Nice going, Micco.*

"Ours is bad, but not that bad," he heard the man remark. "I think I'll pass."

The other man returned, and Tommy heard the exchange of the tape and thanks from Micco.

The boat rocked as they climbed back into their own craft. Tommy heard their shouted goodbyes and then their boat racing off. He waited, using all his self-discipline to avoid bolting through the door. Finally, he heard Micco shout "Coast is clear."

He pushed the head door open and climbed back up the stairs to lie on the deck, breathing, looking up into the black night speckled with pinhole stars, happy to be alive. *I have a job to do, and I'm still on track. This is my destiny.*

When he had recovered, he went back up to the pilothouse to join Micco. "That was some fast thinking, Micco. I'm impressed."

"We natives have it built into our DNA. It was rough trying to survive you white men."

"You get no argument from me there. The things that happened to blacks, Jews, and other groups not only in this country but around the world, was horrible. But what we did to the Indians doesn't get enough exposure."

"Natives. We don't like 'Indians' or 'Native Americans.' My people, the Seminole tribe, we had a good home here in Florida. Then the Spanish came, and it wasn't so bad for a while—we traded and got along somewhat. When the 'American' settlers came, we were pushed onto reservations here. Then after they decided they needed this land, we were shipped away to the Midwest. There were countless promises made and broken by the United States government."

"I'm ashamed of that. It's horrible," Tommy said.

"Horrible is right. Our women were raped and taken from their families as sex slaves. Women and children were slaughtered, as well as innocent men who were just farmers. They gave us diseases we had no immunity to. They took away our worship of the earth and nature, and forced their bizarre Christian religion on us—brainwashed our children with it."

Tommy heard the anger building in Micco's voice. "They took our culture, forcing us to learn English and adopt their customs and dress. Pushed their alcohol on us to make us weak, stupid, and dependent.

"We had always respected the earth and wasted nothing. We watched them rape and pillage every natural resource. They killed animals, who have better spirits than man, just for fun. We're still watching them do it to this day, sucking the oil, gasses, and minerals from the Earth and hunting innocent beasts for pleasure."

"It's ironic," Tommy said. "Most of those are things we accuse the 'savages' in the Middle East of doing today. History does repeat. We never learn, as a species, despite the scientific progress we make."

Micco scoffed. "One day a guy from New York stopped by my stall on the way to Key West. He was complaining that he was at the Walmart up in Key Largo and nobody was speaking English anymore. I imagined my ancestors coming back to the teepee after visiting the trading post a few hundred years ago, complaining about the same sort of thing."

Tommy laughed. "Right. What goes around, comes around. One thing that makes me sick though," he said, "is this guy Brand who wants to be president—and his hero is Andrew Jackson."

Micco spit at the mention of the name. "Jackson was the greatest betrayer and slaughterer of my people. The worst of them—back then anyway. Brand is the worst of men today. Maybe he's Jackson's evil spirit come back again. I fear for everything that's left if he's elected."

Tommy wanted to say more, but feared he'd tip Micco off. *He's sharp. Maybe I'll be his hero in a few weeks.*

He looked out over the darkened ocean and considered the peace and power of the massive body of water surrounding them. He thought about the beauty of the many forms of life living beneath their boat and he wondered how much man-made garbage was down there, violating the creatures and their natural environment. He thought of a documentary he'd watched recently, in which they'd shown aerial shots of miles of plastic and garbage formed together on the sea, and it saddened him.

"Your people had it right, Micco. Respect for the earth."

"That was our creed. The earth and nature were our gods. We only took what we needed, and we prayed over the animals we had to kill to survive. No part of the kill went unused."

"Like the Asians," Tommy said, thinking of his friend Sensei Molletier and what the man had taught him about his culture of respect and dignity. "I don't know how mankind changed from that to what we have now."

"They took this land from us, but nature will take it back from them if they keep abusing it."

Tommy went below to get his things together for a quick disembarkment when they reached Miami. When he came back to the pilothouse, Micco removed a thick stamped-copper bracelet from his wrist and gave it to him. "Take this, from my people. It's old. It will help you on your journey, whatever that is."

Tommy thanked him and placed it on his wrist. He held it up to the cabin's dome light to inspect it. "It's beautiful. Is it symbolic?"

"Yes. To my people, the arrow is an important symbol. It stands for our ability to hunt our prey, and defend ourselves against our enemies in times of war. If the arrow points to the left, it helps to ward off evil. To the right means war."

I'll need both of those, Tommy thought. He made sure that the arrow was pointing to the left, at least temporarily.

Micco motioned past the bow. "Lights ahead; there's Miami in the distance. We'll be there soon."

18 MOTEL HELL

TOMMY PAID THE CLERK behind the bullet-proof glass using cash. He tried to keep his face down, obscuring it with the bill of the ball cap that he wore pulled down low on his head. He raised his walking stick in thanks and took the key she slid into the metal tray. It was a regular door key, attached to a diamond-shaped plastic fob with the name of the seedy motel and room number, which had been mostly erased over time. *Haven't seen one of these in a long time. Old school. Better days.*

He left the office and rounded the corner, following the arrows painted on the walls to where his room was located.

"Need anything?" he heard a voice ask.

He peered into an enclosure to his left, having difficulty seeing in the darkness through the over-sized cheap sunglasses he was wearing. In the glow of soda and candy vending machines inside, he saw a thin, shirtless white man leaning against the wall. He ignored the man but entered to buy a few bottles of water, hoping that the sickness he was feeling was from dehydration.

The man spoke again. "I got whatever you need, gramps. Need some dope? Want a blow-job?"

Tommy ignored him, lowering his sea bag to the floor and examined the choices in the machine.

"How about some ass?" the man persisted. "I got nothin' on under these shorts. You can do me quick. Twenty bucks and you're in, old-timer. Real quick. Nobody's around. Unless you got a room. Fifty then, for an hour, if you need the time to get it up."

Tommy selected a bill from his wallet and inserted it to make his purchase. As he expected, the man made a grab for the wallet. He quickly moved it out of reach with one hand, while grabbing the man's wrist with the other. He used it as leverage to twist the man around, facing away from him, and brought the walking stick up and under the man's chin.

He squeezed it tight against the man's throat, slamming him face-first into the vending machine, cracking one of the brightly painted beverage buttons. A bottle of soda tumbled down the chute.

"Damn it, I wanted water, you son of a bitch," Tommy said.

The man gurgled and struggled for breath. Tommy felt his adrenaline and anger surge. He knew if he kept it up just a few moments more, the man might be lost, along with his plans. *Who knows what brought this poor bastard to this place in his life.* He swung the man around, releasing him and shoving him out of the vending area.

The man stared at him in shock, eyes bulging and gasping for breath. He held his neck as blood ran down his forehead. Tommy took a step toward him, and the man turned and ran. *So much for keeping a low profile.* He completed his purchase of two bottles of water and continued to make his way down the last stretch to his room.

As he passed a door, it opened behind him, and he heard another voice.

"Hello, good-looking."

He turned around to see an obese woman leaning against the doorway. Homemade tattoos ran down the length of her arms, and her polyester one-piece dress was stretched to its limits, flesh bulging out at the seams of her arms and cleavage.

Jesus Christ. It's one-stop shopping here. "No thanks, lady."

"Your loss, buster. You know where to find me if you change your mind."

He reached the room and had to work the key for a while to get it to turn the lock. He noticed the room's window was badly cracked, and had been patched over with old newspaper.

As he stepped in, the scent of cheap deodorizer filled his nostrils. Past that, further into the room, was an underlying odor of mildew. The bed leaned down at one corner, and when he pulled up the thin sheet covering it he saw the end of a broken-off pool cue substituting for its leg. He set his sea bag upright on an injured vinyl chair.

Removing his firearm from the bag, he slid open the nightstand drawer to deposit it. He noticed the Gideon's Bible sitting inside, and pulled it out. It fell open in his hands to a page that had a business card for a local massage parlor stuck in it. A passage on the page immediately caught his eye.

"Neither shall he regard the God of his fathers, nor the desire of women, nor regard any god: for he shall magnify himself above all."

That's Brand alright. I'm getting omens now; I must be on the right track. It matches what Moses told me on the beach. Brand's the fucking anti-Christ.

He needed to piss. The smell of stale urine met him in the bathroom, and the tub and sink fixtures were rusty and dripping. A translucent used condom stuck to the bottom of the trash can.

He emptied himself into the toilet, and the handle fell off when he tried to flush it. He retrieved it, using a coin to screw it back on. Unwrapping a bar of soap, he found it already soggy, and washed his hands carefully, using the hottest water he could tolerate.

Exiting the bathroom, he lay down carefully on the bed, which made a variety of noises to greet his arrival. He picked up the remote control on the side table and turned on the television. It burst to life with the morning news and coverage of Brand's upcoming veteran's event. *At least the TV works.*

A woman named Brenda was talking about the event. "The veterans are lining up to support Mr. Brand. They just love him and want to be around him. They know that he stands for strength and honor for our country." *Bullshit, lady. He's a draft-dodger. We all know that. You're lying, just like he does.*

The long night on the boat had exhausted him, and he rolled over to sleep. As he did, he felt it—a sharp pain. He probed under his ribs, pressing with three fingers until he hit the right spot, and the pain replayed. He knew. *It's back. There's not much time now.*

19 PERFORMANCE ART

CATHERINE BRAND READIED herself for bed. As she leaned toward the bathroom mirror, the phone rang, causing her to jump and smear her eyeliner. She picked up the handset. "Hi, Mom."

"He's due back in town tonight, isn't he?" her mother asked on the other end of the line.

"Yes, Mom. He's been gone for ten days, so you know what that means for me. I'm getting myself ready now. Hopefully, he's too plastered to want to try. I can't take this crazy shit much longer. I'm going to wait until he's in a good mood some day and ask him if we can't just discreetly hire a prostitute."

"Why don't you just leave, honey? Why don't you just leave him? You could go back to your career. You were at the top. You had the best roles on Broadway before that monster came into your life and ruined it."

"You know it's a lot more complicated than that. Not during this campaign. I should have left him before all of this, but it's just not possible now. Maybe after he loses, and I hope to God he does. If not, I've got at least four years of this ridiculous routine and putting on a happy face in public."

"It's abuse. It's sexual and psychological abuse. You should leak what that goddamn pervert does to the media. And that he hits you sometimes if it doesn't go well."

"It's only you, me, and him that know that, Mom. I only told you in case something happens to me some day, and you promised me you would never leak it. If it gets out, one of us is probably going to die."

"Well, I hope he has a heart attack then, the filthy bastard."

"Maybe I can help him with that tonight, with any luck. I love you, Mom. I've got to go."

She returned to her rigorous routine, first correcting the mistake in her eyeliner. Her makeup had to be applied just right. Thomas would pick up on any discrepancy and fly into a rage, saying it was all ruined and it was her fault that he couldn't perform. When she finished, she checked and double-checked every detail of the gaudy, overdone lipstick, eyelashes, eyeliner, and rouge.

Next, she began the part she hated most. She opened a drawer and pulled out a tray of 1950s rubber hair curlers. She wound each one tightly and carefully into place. When she was through, she put a hair-net over them and checked again in the mirror. *I look fucking ridiculous.*

She prepared her body for an assault on her flesh that she hoped wouldn't come, then returned to the bedroom and opened a drawer. She withdrew a pair of vintage red flannel pajamas and dressed in them. Lastly, she pulled back the covers and slid into bed, hoping for the best.

While she tried to sleep, she went back over what had gotten her to this point in her life.

Mom's right. I could've had everything on my own, but I took a chance to try to get those things the easy way. I should've had more confidence in myself. I swore I'd always be independent of any man; I would never be controlled. Now look at me—pathetic. How was I to know, though? He was charming and funny. He hid his ego well in those early days. I had no idea what a freak he was. I made the wrong choice.

She thought about what she'd said to her mother and played assassination scenarios through her mind to help keep her sanity. *If someone would do that for me, I'd be free. And the country could escape a monster if he somehow manages to pull this damn thing off.*

~*~

She woke when she heard the bedroom door close, and saw him pass by in the dark on his way to the bathroom. He cursed and banged things around, and she knew it wasn't going to go smoothly. She closed her eyes again, hoping to get back to sleep. *He always knows when I'm faking.* She prayed that he would come out and get into the bed and just go to sleep without bothering. *I'll know as soon as that door opens.*

The bathroom door creaked open slightly, and he began. "Mommy? Are you there? It's me. I'm home now."

Shit. Catherine began her part in the charade. "Thomas? You're late. It's past curfew and well past your bedtime. Come here, young man."

He crept to the bed, naked and cowering. "I'm sorry, Ma. I tried to get home on time, Ma." He went around to his side and got into the bed.

She sat up. "Let me smell you, Thomas. Open your mouth and breathe, young man."

He leaned over to her and did as she asked.

The stench was overwhelming, and she almost gagged and ruined the charade. She slapped him hard on the face. "You're drunk, Thomas. You know that Mommy doesn't like you to drink. You're too young. You'll ruin your life. You're very bad, Thomas."

He whimpered. "Don't hit me, Mommy. Please don't hit me."

She could hear him rubbing himself, getting himself ready. She slapped him a second time, per the script. "You're bad. Worthless."

"I said don't hit me, Mommy!" he screamed. He shoved her down, yanked off her pajama bottoms, and then flipped her over. He pulled her up on her knees, then pulled her legs apart and tried to enter her. He pushed and attempted to guide himself, but she could tell he was still only halfway there. *He's too damn drunk to get it up, again.*

He became more frustrated, breaking the protocol slightly by cursing himself. He alternately tried to stimulate himself and rub against her, but to no avail. As she expected, he gave up and rolled back over on the bed on his stomach, crying. "Then punish me, Mommy. Go ahead, punish me. I deserve it."

She reached over and slid open the nightstand drawer to remove the strap-on and lubricant. She copied his earlier steps, beginning by pulling him up on his knees.

She went at him furiously, reaching around to find him now erect. He was spent within a minute, and rolled over to sleep without saying a word.

Now that part I don't mind. Catherine smiled and headed to the bathroom to shower.

20 SHOPPING

THIS IS THE PLACE, just up ahead," the taxi driver said to Tommy. "Medical supply, right?"

"You got it, boss." Tommy paid the man, leaving a generous tip. He exited and went into the store.

"Where's the wheelchair section?" he asked the young clerk behind the register.

He followed the clerk's guidance and looked over the selection.

The clerk followed him over. "We've got some great motorized models…"

"Not interested," Tommy cut him off. "Self-propelled only." He sat in a few of them, gauging their comfort and, more importantly, each one's ability to conceal.

When he'd narrowed the selection down, he rolled up and down the aisle in each, varying his speed. He tried some quick exits, jumping up out of them, eliminating the ones that were too obstructive. After one such drill, he doubled over, winded and in pain.

The clerk watched him suspiciously. "You need an ambulance or something, mister?"

"No," Tommy responded.

He finally found just the right one and wheeled himself up to the register in it. "I like this one. What about accessories? How do I carry my crap around?"

The clerk showed him a few tiller bags, including one that was designed to hang from the front, behind his legs.

"That one's perfect. I'll take it," Tommy said.

The clerk rang up the sale. "You don't seem like you need a wheelchair," he said.

Tommy was annoyed at the invasive comment. "My condition gets worse every day. Mind your business, kid. Or you might need one." He paid in cash, then sat in the wheelchair.

"Now call me one of those handicapped taxis that can handle this thing."

~*~

The dank Army/Navy store was full of memories. Tommy wheeled himself down the aisles, stopping to reminisce each time he saw an item that he had known or used so long ago. *It seems like another lifetime.*

"Help you, bub?" a grizzled old man said, approaching from the head of the aisle.

"Yeah," Tommy said. "I'm going to the veteran's thing that Brand is having. All my stuff was lost in a fire a long time ago. I need to replace my uniform and medals."

"Damn, ain't you a lucky one. How the hell did you swing that? He's one fine man. I wish I could get in on that. I'd like to shake his hand and thank him personally for standing up to these goddamn liberals and saying what needs to be said about all the fucking faggots, darkies, and foreigners that are taking over our country."

Tommy worked hard to restrain himself. *Don't make a scene and blow it. Go along with him. Keep a low profile.* "Just lucky, like you said. And damn straight about all that scum."

"So, what can I do you for? What branch, which conflict were you?"

"Marines. 'Nam. Between '67 and '69. I had a Purple Heart, Bronze Star, and a few other pins and medals."

"I've got replicas of those, sure. I can help you with all that. Over here's the Marine stuff from around then, as far as uniforms. You probably want dress blues for this event, it's high class and all."

"Yeah, for sure," Tommy replied. He browsed through the racks from his wheelchair, annoyed that the man continued to hover over him.

"Listen, bub," the shop owner continued. "You seem to be a guy like me. Proud of this country, proud of our service, proud of our heritage. Our *white* heritage. You down with that? Because if you are, we have a little group you might be interested in. We're old-timers, so we don't give a shit. We're sort of the radical arm of the Brand Brigade." He cackled at his own comment.

Tommy paused and thought for a moment. "Damn right, pal. What's happening to our country is bullshit. I'm new around here—just retired. I've come down to get out of the cold, and I have plenty of time on my hands. I'm sick though, so I have a short runway. That makes me dangerous, if you know what I mean. Give me the skinny."

They shook hands. "My name's Ralph. We have a meetup coming. We use the back room here, after closing. There's going to be a lot of those types I mentioned protesting the Brand event, like always. We're gonna make a statement. I got my hands on some C-4 and a blast cap, but it's dangerous shit, and nobody in our group knows how to work with it."

"I'm Tommy. I'm your guy, then. I had my EOD—the crab badge. I was our unit's ordinance man."

The man smiled happily. "Ain't that something! See, karma *is* real. Here you come rollin' in here, just what we're looking for." He slapped Tommy on the shoulder.

"Damn right," Tommy responded. "Karma sure is something." *As you'll soon find out, asshole.*

He wheeled down the aisles with his new friend until he had everything he needed.

As he checked out, he asked, "Two more things. Is there one of those places around here where I can get a temporary pay-as-you-go cell phone? I don't have a phone in my new place, and I figured I'd try that. Also, where's the nearest liquor store?"

Both places were within the adjacent downtown blocks. The man wrote him directions and agreed to hold his items until he came back for them.

The cell phone purchase was straightforward and discreet. Afterward, Tommy wheeled himself down the street to the liquor store and entered.

"What's the best bourbon you have?" he asked the clerk.

"Not long ago," she said, leaning down toward him from behind the counter, "we got a bottle of Martin Mills 24 Year. It's legendary stuff, and very rare. It's tough to sell around here though—$500 a bottle is too rich for most folks. It came out in 1999 after someone found an old cask. There are only a few hundred bottles in the world."

"Yeah," said another patron. "And a lot of fakes. It's the Bigfoot of bourbon. Don't get screwed, buddy, it's probably counterfeit."

"It sounds perfect," Tommy said. *This should make for a nice bribe to get where I need to go.* "I'll take it."

~*~

Back in his room, he tried to step out of the wheelchair and found the effort difficult, requiring two attempts. His knees buckled, and his arms failed to push his own weight up and out. When he finally rose, he found himself winded and lay down on the bed before he could unpack his purchases from the bags that hung from the handles.

Waking hours later, he still felt exhausted and became concerned that his breathing was still labored. Thinking it might be due to the increased heat and humidity, he reached over and turned the dial on the window air conditioner next to his bed.

After lying still for a time, hoping it would go away, he began to panic. *Time to break out the heavy weapons. About a week left, and I need to be stronger.*

He went to the sea bag and retrieved a plastic case. He opened it, exposing several small syringes—the steroid injections prescribed by Dr. Mason, which he had saved for this time he knew would come. *One a day for the rest of the way out should get me through.*

He took one and injected himself, then opened a bottle of B12 vitamins, took several, and placed the bottle next to the others he took each day.

21 QUESTIONERS

BUSINESS AT THE MARKET was slow. Life seemed empty since Tommy had left. Tara still hadn't recovered, and she missed him badly. She sat in her stall at the farmer's market with Whitey on her lap.

"He'll come back, buddy. He hinted he would. He's just got something to take care of, he said. And he'll come back to us. I know he will, Whitey."

The dog looked up at her and licked her arm. She rose and put him down to get back to work. Micco passed by, and she shouted a greeting to him.

"Any news on your beau?" he stopped to ask.

"No, Micco. Just the vague letter he left. He had something to do before he got too sick. He'll be back, I know it. I just know it."

"I hope so, Tara. I liked that guy, and he bought lots of fish. Did he give any hint how he got out of here or where he went?"

"No. Hopefully he didn't go far, and we'll see him back around soon."

They both went about their business. Traffic picked up, and it helped to pass the time. When the day drew near its end, she walked outside the stall to stretch. Looking down the row of other stands, she noticed two men in suits. They were talking to Micco, and one was holding up a badge.

She casually walked back into the stall and stashed Whitey in the back room. She gave the dog a treat and filled his water bowl. "Now keep quiet, Whitey. Please. It's important."

She went back into the stall and began sorting through her products, placing the ones that were no longer saleable into a burlap sack. She glanced down the row again. The men were now at Mrs. Park's booth, and she was out front with them, talking animatedly. Tara saw her motion in her stall's direction and ducked back out of sight before the men could turn to follow the gesture.

I've got to think, quickly.

She continued to sort until she turned and found them facing her. "Hello, handsome gentlemen. Care for some fresh organic fruit? It's got none of that poison in it that the stuff from the grocery store has. I have free samples, what do you think?"

They waited through her comments, humorless. One of them held up the badge. "We're with the FBI. We're looking for a man who might have passed through this way, or could still be in the area."

The other man held up a picture of Tommy. It appeared to be a picture taken when he retired, as he was still in uniform. He was close to the same age, but well-groomed and far better for wear and tear than the Tommy she knew.

"Wow. Yep, that's Tommy alright. He was here for a few days. Then, like most who pass through, he was gone. We get a lot of that—

vacationers, vagabonds, retirees on their way down to Key West.”

"How well did you know him, ma'am?"

She knew it was a trick question, and her response would have to match up with whatever the other vendors had told them. She knew they had all seen her and Tommy together. She stayed in character.

"Look, sugar. Like I said, they come, and they go. I'm kinda flirtatious; it helps to sell the goods, if you know what I mean. Fruits and veggies, veggies and fruits.

"The guy was around for a few days, we hung out a little. Nothing serious. Then he split. At least that's what I'm guessing. I haven't seen him in a few days. I suppose he could still be around, and just not hungry for what I'm selling. He didn't say much about himself. Didn't say where he was going. Didn't say goodbye at all, actually. Now, how about some of these ripe, delicious melons, fellas?"

They looked at each other, then thanked her for her help and continued on to the next stall.

~*~

Another day passed, and it still hurt, surprisingly. *Maybe he's not coming back.* She lay on her bed in the early morning, trying to convince herself to rise and lead the tai chi class on the beach. It was hard to do anything without thinking about him, reliving their short list of memories, and wondering where he was and whether he was okay.

As she often did, she replayed their perfect days together just before he left. She wished they had a lifetime of days like that. Perhaps they would, in the hereafter, as he had mused while they sat on the beach the night they drank the peyote tea.

The phone rang, and she rose to answer it. Whitey jumped out of her way and quickly moved to lie on the warm spot she'd vacated, laying his head on her pillow. "Let's see, will it be the mother or the child this time," she said to herself as she picked up the receiver.

"Hey, I love you," he said.

She fell back onto the bed, remembering Whitey at the last minute, just missing him. "Tommy. I love you. Please come back."

"I will…I'll try. You were right about the medicine, Tara. I'm going downhill. I feel it more every day. My stamina is failing, and I'm hurting. I'm sick, Tara. I wish I could do everything over and have a life with you. But I'm gonna try to get back there."

"Be careful, Tommy. The FBI was looking around here, asking about you. I'm sure they have a lot going on besides that, and they were a couple of young guys who seemed to just be going through the motions. But you should know they're on your trail."

"Damn it. Alright, I don't need much more time. I'll tell you what. I'll signal you, and we'll meet back on the small key we stayed at. If I can make it, that is."

"You will, Tommy. I know you will. Please come back to me soon."

"It's all I want right now," he said. "I can't call you again if they've been around looking for me. It'll take them another day or so, but they'll probably tap your line if they think we're involved. I'm using disposable phones, but they could still record every conversation you have. Be careful. I love you."

The line went dead, and she rolled over and buried her face in the pillow.

22 CAMPAIGN HQ

CHAOS RULED as the campaign team scrambled to set up their office space for the event, with only days remaining. The advance team had done a good job, but much was left to be accomplished in the remaining stretch.

Brenda ducked into her office for a break from the noise. She saw Stinson passing by and motioned him to join her. He came in, closing the door behind him.

"How're we looking, Harry?" she asked.

"The usual. It's mayhem, but we'll get there. When's Brand getting in?"

"Tomorrow," she answered. "We need to keep him sober and focused. He can't screw this veteran's event up. It's the big leagues now, just us and the Democrats, and they're far more experienced at campaigning."

"Chaos has always seems to work in our favor," Stinson said. "It's like this guy has some kind of evil guiding force."

"Yeah. I just hope that's not us."

They were interrupted by a young aide knocking on the glass. Brenda motioned her in.

"There's some old guy in a wheelchair out there," the aide said. "He's asking for you, Brenda. He's out in the reception area by the elevators."

"I'll go see what this is about, Harry. Let's get together at lunch and do a checkpoint on our to-do list."

They both rose and left the office. Brenda made her way out into the lobby area. The receptionist motioned to a white-bearded man in a wheelchair. He wore a baseball hat with "US Marine Corps" and "Vietnam Veteran" stitched on it, and oversized senior-citizen sunglasses. He had a blanket placed on his lap, covering his legs. A paper bag sat on the blanket. There was something about him; her intuition tingled. He reminded her very much of her own late father, who had also been a Marine and Vietnam vet. *God bless these guys, they've been through hell for this country. This one would look great on stage next to Brand.*

She approached. "Hello, sir. I'm Brenda Holloway, Mr. Brand's campaign manager. How can I help you?"

He looked up at her. "My name is Tommy Domingo. I'm a big supporter of Mr. Brand. I wrote you a letter."

She remembered the letter immediately. "Oh, Mr. Domingo. Yes, I did receive that. I believe we responded...or meant to, anyway. Things have been crazy. I had to mail a letter out to you. I didn't see any telephone information in yours, or someone would have called immediately."

"Yes," he answered. "I forgot to put it on there. My brain's not what it was. Agent Orange and all that. I'd really like to be part of the event. I brought something to help bribe Mr. Brand," he laughed. "It's very rare and expensive—my favorite, but I can't afford it for myself."

He handed the bag to her, and she slid a box out of it. *Oh shit. Brand definitely doesn't need this.*

This poor guy probably spent his whole social security check on it. I can't just throw it away or give it to someone else. I better think of something good.

"Oh, that's so sweet of you, Mr. Domingo. But we can't accept alcohol—campaign rules and regulations prevent it. I think Mr. Brand would be happy to know that you enjoyed it yourself."

She saw the disappointment on his face. "In fact, perhaps you can tell him yourself. We're interested in making you a part of this event, as one of the veterans on stage with Mr. Brand at the rally. I believe one of our staff was just working on the background verifications for everyone as the last step. Hold on, while I check on that."

"Oh," he said. "I hope he can find mine. There was a fire at the VA back home, and a lot of records were destroyed. They're trying to rebuild them electronically, but don't even get me started on the VA. It's a nightmare, dealing with them."

She took the opportunity to return the bottle to him, and she returned to the office area. She found Stinson huddled over his laptop at a cubicle toward the back of the room.

"Harry, what's the deal with the checks on these vets? One of them is here, and I'd like to let him know where he stands if I can."

Stinson rattled the keyboard with his fingers, then scanned a spreadsheet. "Which one?" he asked.

"Domingo. Thomas Domingo."

"I haven't been able to find anything on him. He's the only one left that we have to verify, in fact."

"Alright, well, he's right out there in the lobby. Adorable old guy, for a Marine, that is. He's okay. He was worried because his records are all screwed up. There was some kind of fire at the VA near his home. Just give me a pass and welcome packet for him and mark that task as complete. At least we finished something today."

"It's your call," Stinson said. He pulled the packet from a file cabinet and handed it to her.

She returned to the lobby and found Domingo waiting. "Mr. Domingo, thank you for being patient. I was able to sort everything out. Here are your packet and pass. Read everything carefully, and follow the instructions to the letter. Security will be tight."

The man smiled. "Thank you, Brenda. This means so much to me. Hey, one more thing. I have a hell of a time getting around in places like that in this buggy. Could I go to the place before the event and scope it out?"

"Oh, sure," she said. "We have people there pretty much full-time these last few days. Just show your pass to the security team. I'll let them know to expect you. Be careful though, it's chaotic. You're officially a guest of honor, Mr. Domingo. Thank you for your service to our country."

They shook hands again, and the man rolled off toward the elevators.

Poor guy. That felt good, my good deed for the day, Brenda thought to herself.

23 PREPARATIONS

TOMMY ROLLED out of the handicap taxi van and continued to the event center. Workers were scurrying around, going in and out of the gaping entrance, carrying scaffolding, lighting, stage decorations, and other large items on forklifts.

He repositioned the badge hanging around his neck and scanned for the employee entrance. He found it, then waited for the most opportune moment to move inside without being stopped. Soon, he found his opening. He rolled over, and a security guard opened the door for him.

"Thanks, buddy," Tommy said, holding his pass out.

"Better grab a hard hat," the guard responded, pulling one from a stack for him.

Tommy placed it over his baseball cap and continued on. He used the elevator to get to the concourse level, then surveyed the stage from his vantage point.

He had found that as a disabled person, he was invisible and people would leave him alone. As long as he kept the badge prominent and acted as if he had business there, nobody challenged him. *I'm sure it will be different tomorrow, at the main event.*

He made his way down to the stage area, and then backstage. *Now I'm getting somewhere.* He stopped, winded and in pain. He was no longer able to physically exert himself for more than a short period of time, and the pain in various parts of his body had grown excruciating at times. *It's growing within me. All over within me.*

A middle-aged woman with a clipboard in her hand approached him.

"Excuse me, sir," she said in a melodic voice. "What are you doing wandering around here all by yourself?"

He tried to recover and think quickly. "I'm a vet, and I'm going to be here tomorrow for the Brand event. I just get nervous about the layout, being in this chair and all. I got kind of a condition, actually a couple of them. I've got to be comfortable with everything in advance." He waited for her response, hoping she wouldn't involve security. *The last thing I need is to be searched. If they do that, I'm done.*

She smiled at him. "I can tell how excited you are. Probably almost as excited as me! I just worship Mr. Brand, and I hope I get the chance to meet him. Oh, my God how amazing would that be?" She squealed with glee at the thought.

"Yeah," Tommy said. "That would be amazing. I'm hoping to meet him, too." *And take him out.*

"Tell you what, young man," she said. "I'm Gloria. I'm in charge of this area. I'll give you the tour myself. Then you'll be right at home tomorrow."

Tommy brightened. "That would be perfect. Thank you, ma'am."

She took him to the stage and the various auxiliary areas that were used for performers and events that took place regularly at the venue. They entered a large room that was being elaborately decorated with obscenely large pictures of

Brand. "This is going to be the staging room. It's where you and the other vets are going to be holding while you wait to go out onto the stage. Mr. Brand will be coming in here to do a private meet-and-greet with all of you before the whole thing starts. Isn't that exciting?"

"It certainly is," Tommy said. He scanned every detail, making mental notes. "Excuse me, do you think I could ah, use the facilities?"

"Certainly. They're right there through that door."

Wheeling himself into the holding area's men's room, he scrutinized its layout. He rolled to the large handicapped stall and pushed his way into it. *I always used the handicapped one for its extra space; now I need it.*

He got up slowly from the wheelchair and unzipped the tiller bag, carefully withdrawing a heavy-duty plastic storage bag. Inside of it was another bag, and inside of that bag was a black semi-automatic handgun, fully loaded with an extended clip. *This should keep it dry.*

He turned back to remove the tank lid and froze. *Oh, shit. It's tankless.* He hurriedly replaced the gun in his tiller bag, flushed the toilet and wheeled himself back into the holding room. His mind was racing; he was panicking. He tried to think and realized something was wrong—his thoughts wouldn't come in an organized manner. *Oh my God, it's even in my brain again.* He thought back to the seizure he'd had in the park not so long ago. *I can't afford that now. Just a little longer. Please, just give me a few more days.*

He rolled back out to the hallway, where Gloria was writing on her clipboard. "Sorry," he said. "Everything takes longer than it used to, especially in this thing. I'm still getting used to it."

"That's okay, sir. Thank you for serving our country. I'm sorry though, but I don't have much more time. I want to show you one more thing. Something very special—the green room."

She took him back into the hallway and then to the room next to the one they'd just been in. "I'm sure you can tell whose room this is!" she said excitedly.

The room was elaborately appointed, with expensive new carpeting and wood and leather furniture. There was a large walnut bar set up. He noticed the entrance to what he thought was a private restroom. "Wow, it's amazing. It's like we're in his own lavish penthouse apartment," Tommy said.

"Yep. I can just imagine myself living here with him. Servants and all that. Another bourbon, Mrs. Brand?" she laughed.

He was still trying to engage and stall her while he tried to think. He noticed that the room had a private lavatory. He pointed to it. "Listen, I'm sorry to be a pain in the ass. I don't feel well. Do you mind if I go one more time? Then I'll get out of your hair."

She hesitated. "I better take you back next door. I don't think anyone but the king should go in here! They probably replaced the toilets with gold-plated ones," she laughed again.

"Yeah, but I don't think I'll make it, seriously. It's an emergency, and I don't want to mess up this carpet."

"Oh, goodness," she said quickly. "Yes, please, hurry then." She rolled him over to the entrance and held the door open for him.

He entered and surveyed the room. It was set up like a residential bathroom, and it looked like some of the fixtures had just been replaced in anticipation of Brand's arrival. There were no stalls, just a lone toilet with a water tank.

Relieved, he checked to make sure the door was locked, then got out of the wheelchair and retrieved the gun from the tiller bag. He opened the tank and carefully placed the plastic bag containing the gun into the water, then replaced the tank cover. *See you tomorrow, friend.*

He flushed the toilet and ran the sink for effect, then exited the room.

She greeted him on the other side, looking anxious. "I'll tell you a little secret—I've done it too," she said. "Number two. It's strange, the little ways we try to connect ourselves to greatness."

"Thanks so much," Tommy said. "I don't want to take up any more of your time. I have a doctor's appointment."

He was feeling very weak, and allowed her to push him back to the employee entrance. He felt that, in that one small concession, he had given in, accepted what was happening to him, although it still seemed surreal. He still found himself thinking of his disease as something temporary—like a flu that he would eventually recover from.

He used his cell phone to summon the taxi van again, and while he waited, he tried to figure out how to adapt the plan to the new circumstances. *How the hell am I going to get into Brand's personal shitter tomorrow?*

24 MEET AND GREET

FTER A LONG, RESTLESS afternoon nap filled with both horrible and blissful dreams, Tommy forced his eyes to open. He focused on the smoke-stained ceiling of his cheap motel room. Examining its water stains, he imagined the bathtub from the floor above crashing down onto him. *What a way to go, after all this.*

He'd slept far longer than he'd intended to. The pain that was slowly creeping through every part of his body was more subdued when he slept and remained still.

At times, he was tempted to lie in bed until it was over. It seemed that all was lost; that in just a week he was no longer physically or mentally capable of pulling off this one last deed for the world before he checked out.

Tommy thought about Tara and wondered what she was doing at that very moment. As he often did now, in these times of self-pity, he began to replay the mistakes he'd made in life and how he wished he could undo each of them. It brought him to the tortured life of his son Bobby, the tortured life of people like Moses, and the homeless man he had met while serving Thanksgiving dinner to those less fortunate.

All those regrets reminded him of his mission. Brand stood for everything he hated about the people who treated others that way. For many of them, Brand was their hero, the leader of their hateful cause. *I'll cut the head off the snake, is what I'll do.*

That brought him to the meeting he was supposed to attend that night, in the back of the Army/Navy store, with a group of white supremacists, and it gave him the energy he needed to get up from the bed and get himself ready. *Ready for battle.*

He rose from the bed, fighting off the pain and pity, feeling like Lazarus as he got to his feet.

I can do this. I have *to do this.* He made his way slowly to his pills and took them, doubling up on the ones for pain. Unable to stand up long enough to shower, he used the bathtub. He dressed slowly, in excruciating pain, then fell into the wheelchair and picked up the phone to call the taxi van. *This fucking thing was supposed to be a prop. Now it's a necessity.*

The van arrived as he waited by the motel office. It was the same driver—a middle-aged black guy who liked to wear his hat sideways.

The man was always helpful and courteous to Tommy, making sure that he was properly loaded, secure, and comfortable before moving on. *He's always respectful to me, yet I ignore him. Why?*

Tommy philosophized, reaching deep into the psyche of his former and current self. He realized there was a time when he would have disliked the man just because he wore his hat differently—because it wasn't on 'right.'

Why should he have to conform to my way of wearing a hat? How important is that, really? Or the type of music I like, or the way I speak. It's ignorant. I was always the ignorant one, and I never realized it until the last few years. People don't understand—it's all in how you choose to look at things.

Now when he saw someone like this, he decided instead to see them as people who had been crapped on their entire lives. Hard-working people who never really had much of a shot. People who would always struggle and probably never have a nice vacation, home, or car. People who would be passed over for opportunity after opportunity in favor of someone who looked 'right.'

"Hey, I don't think I ever asked your name," Tommy called to him from the back of the van.

The man glanced in the rearview mirror, looking surprised. "Taquan. Some friends call me TQ."

"How ya doing, TQ? I'm Tommy. I'm sorry I haven't been very friendly on these trips. I got a lot on my mind, and I'm kinda sick, you know?"

"I think we all got a lot on our mind these days, sir."

"Call me Tommy."

"Tommy. Sorry," TQ said.

"You talking about Brand?"

"Yeah, but I don't like to get into the politics with my passengers. Turns out bad."

"Alright. Well, I'm no fan, TQ. The man's the goddamn anti-Christ. I believe it. I'm no Bible-thumper, but I've seen the passages about it, and he's the guy."

"Well I am a Bible-thumper, and you're damn sure right. I never thought about it that way. I hope my mom and grandma don't figure that out; they'll be all crazy, yelling about the 'end of days have come.'"

"I always ignored him as much as I can. Now he's one step away, and I'm afraid to ignore him. Good thing the polls show him pretty far behind the Democrat."

"Polls showed him pretty far behind all them Republicans, too," TQ replied.

"Damn if you aren't right. Okay, now I'm more scared."

They laughed as TQ pulled up to the Army/Navy store. Tommy paid him with a generous tip. "Nice talking to you. See you on the return trip, if you're still working."

"I'm always working, Tommy. Always working. Got bills to pay and a daughter who's dreaming about college. Smart kid."

TQ helped him get down the ramp and then drove off. The shop lights were off. Tommy rolled up to the front and peered through the glass. He could see movement inside, and then heard a bolt thrown back on the door. "Come on in," someone said.

The door swung open, and he rolled in. When his eyes adjusted, he saw Ralph and three other men standing by a glass counter drinking coffee from foam cups.

"What's with the wheelchair?" one of the men asked Ralph. "You didn't say the guy was a cripple."

"I have to use it sometimes," Tommy said. "More often than not these days. Anyway, it'll help me with your plan. It hides things, and they don't search them that carefully. And I'm dying, which makes me a dangerous motherfucker, with nothing to lose."

Ralph introduced him to the group. "Fellas, this here's Tommy. Explosives/ordinance specialist. Marine Corps. 'Nam."

A tall, wiry man in a flannel shirt with its sleeves cut off stepped forward.

"What the hell was you and that nigger laughing about out there? I saw you through the window."

Tommy wanted to pull his walking stick from the holder on the side of the chair and take the man's teeth out. "Trying to act normal. It sounds like we have something big to do here. I'm not going to wear my heart on my sleeve and attract attention. Not until after tomorrow."

"Sounds smart to me," Ralph said.

"You're a damn fool, Ralph," the flannel man said. "What the hell are you thinking, bringing in someone new this late? I told you I can handle the C-4. What if he's a goddamn cop or Fed? Don't say my fucking name. I want nothing to do with this guy."

"You calling me a cop?" Tommy challenged him. "Fuck you, pal. I'm on your side. I'm looking to make a difference here, and I ain't got much time left. Cancer. I got nothing to fear and nothing to worry about. You fuck with that C-4 without knowing what you're doing, and you'll blow yourself and your own people to bits."

"Yeah? Well, I was in 'Nam too, buddy. Let's see what you know about C-4. Tell me how us grunts used it sometimes?"

Tommy was silent for a moment. He knew that he knew the answer—it was there somewhere in his addled brain, but he couldn't call it forward. He struggled to summon the memory, and became frustrated, which seemed to push it further away.

The man put his cup down on the counter and confronted Tommy. "See, the motherfucker is a fraud—probably a cop. He should know the answer. What the fuck we gonna do, Ralph? We got to kill him or something. I ain't going to jail for your stupidity, Ralph. I'll shoot this old pile of shit myself."

Just try it, asshole. The diversion was enough for Tommy's brain to work, and the answer came to the surface. "Calm the fuck down, moron. We burned it to cook with sometimes, or to start cooking fires. It burns like wood. Doesn't explode without a blast cap or detonator."

The man stepped away, grumbling. "I still don't trust him."

"Let's go over everything in the back," Ralph said. They all followed him into the rear office.

Tommy listened to the plan. The police had already designated areas outside the convention center for the protesters and Brand Brigade, and both areas would be cordoned off to prevent any mixing of the groups.

"The security team and local police are probably already working with the Feds," Tommy said. "They probably already have a list and pictures of the leaders and prominent folks on both sides. If you guys have been to the rallies, or been active on the internet, especially if you're a hardcore supporter, they probably already know you, and they'll be watching you."

The flannel-shirt man spoke up. "You know what then, buddy? That makes you the perfect person to do the *legwork*. They don't know you at all. You plant the package for us, then."

He laughed at his own mean-spirited joke, and Tommy hated him even more. "I agree. Like

I said, nobody bothers someone in a wheelchair, and I know how to handle the goods."

"I told you he was the right man," Ralph said to the group. They all seemed relieved to have their own roles in the plot diminished.

They sat at the table, going over every detail again and again. Tommy had won the confidence of the other men, who weren't much better than the one wearing the flannel shirt. *Hateful human garbage, all of them. The kind of assholes who would've taunted my kid mercilessly.*

One of them spoke up. "I can't wait to see those sniveling fucking weasels go flyin' through the air." He slapped the table in his excitement.

"This guy can carry the package, but I don't trust him with the detonator," the flannel shirt man said. "I'm keeping control of that like we planned."

"That's fine," Ralph said. "You guys do your thing at the rally; the rest of us will wait here. When the shit hits the fan, come back, and we'll all hole up here for the night."

Satisfied, the group dispersed, leaving only Tommy and Ralph behind.

"Mind if I borrow what I need from the store to finish this up?" Tommy asked.

"Take whatever you need. I'm gonna lay down and get some sleep. Wake me when you're done, and I'll let you out."

Tommy grew sicker and more exhausted as the night went by. He worked alone in the back room to prepare the charge, blast cap, and remote detonator as they had described. When he was through, he woke Ralph.

"I'm done. I'll take the package with me and plant it in the morning when I get there. I have a pass to get in, so I'll have it in place. It'll be right in the middle of the scum, they'll never notice it. I colored and shaped it to blend in with the concrete barriers they have set up."

He handed Ralph a large, older model-mobile phone. "Here's the detonator. Tell your guy to pull up the wire antenna. That part is critical, to cover the distance to the package. Then he should just make like he's placing a phone call. Tell him to enter 666 and press the Send button. There'll be a small delay. Tell him to make sure to act like he's really making a phone call, actually talking to someone, or the cops might get suspicious."

Ralph paid close attention, repeating each step as Tommy recited it.

Tommy used his phone to call for a taxi, then attempted to wheel himself to the door. He found he could barely move the chair—he was spent. Ralph moved behind him and began to push him the rest of the way, and opened the door for him.

"You sure you're gonna be able to do this?" Ralph asked.

"Yeah, no problem," Tommy said. "Long day. Tomorrow the adrenaline will be flowing. Big day."

25 CRAVINGS

THOMAS BRAND PACED the office restlessly. "I'm all right, damn it. I can function. This is bullshit."

His campaign advisers held their ground from around the conference table.

"We're unanimous on this," Brenda said. "Nothing to drink until the rally is over, or we'll quit. If you go out there drunk, it'll be obvious. This isn't the primaries anymore. The klieg lights are on you.

"The media doesn't like you, and they'll have a field day if they know you're drunk. And it's becoming more evident. You're getting out of hand. You're going to blow it, and we all have too much invested, sir. *You* have too much invested."

He strode to her defiantly. "You're talking to me this way? I'll replace you in a heartbeat, young lady."

"You'll have to replace us all," Stinson said meekly.

Brand gave him his staunchest glare. "Oh, Christ. Now the fat guy is talking shit to me. I'll ruin you too, tubby. Get your fat ass up and get me a cup of coffee."

"Brand—the bullying has got to stop, too. We're all on the same team. It's divisive."

Brand turned to see who had spoken. It was Alex Carenton, his wealthiest backer, and someone he could not afford to lose.

Carenton continued. "There's a lot of stress in a campaign. The booze doesn't help. You can certainly get by until after the event tonight. It's only ten fucking hours. Then you and I will have a few at the reception, and get hammered in your suite after that if you want. But we have to make this event a success tonight."

Brand groused and sat back down at the head of the table. "I'm going to hold you to that, Carenton. Alright, what's the status? Let's go around the table."

"Everything is in place," Brenda said. "You don't have a Secret Service detail until next week, so we've beefed up security."

"What? Where's my Secret Service? I'm the nominee."

"It's not normal to have a big event this soon. You asked me to schedule it right away, remember? Also, there will be a significant protest outside, along with our usual large group of supporters."

"Fuck those trouble-making liberal swine," Brand sneered. "My Brand Brigade is going to take care of them, believe me."

Everyone paused. "What are you saying?" Brenda asked. "What do you mean 'going to?'"

He looked around at them. "Never mind. You know what I'm saying. They're bigger, tougher, and they love me. They'll take care of any problems those filthy hippies cause."

"You've got to focus on issues and stop trying to turn everything into a big battle," Carenton said.

"This *is* a goddamn battle," Brand snarled. "Politics is a cesspool. I don't need this bullshit. I never expected to get this far, all I wanted was free publicity for my business and a chance to shit on the Democrats for a while."

"I understand that," Carenton replied. "I think we all know that. But now we're one step away. You can be President of the United States, Thomas. Think about that for a minute. One of the great men in history."

Brand got up again and examined himself in the mirror. "I'm already one of the great men in history. Of business history, anyway. You're right though," he said straightening his tie. "There's only been what, twenty presidents or something? My name would be right up there with them."

The group looked at one another, and Brenda shook her head to warn them not to correct him. A few appeared to be suppressing laughter.

"Exactly," Brenda said. "Right where it be-longs."

"I'll get elected, and we'll cut taxes and create so many goddamn loopholes we'll never pay a cent again. It will be pure profit. I'll get rid of all the fucking red tape and regulations."

"Just be careful," Carenton said. "You'll get pushback. Don't forget that some of those regulations are for safety and environmental concerns. People will get scared."

"Fuck that," Brand said. "Nobody cares about that. Just those idiots on the left. We're winning, so obviously more people are with us. This must be what they want."

"The last item we have on the agenda for this meeting is for you to go through tonight's speech for the group, sir. I think their feedback might be valuable. We might come up with a few last-minute tweaks to make this a big success." Brenda said.

Brand had picked up a remote control from a wall-mounted holder and turned on the meeting room's television. He flipped channels until he found a news station that was showing images of him and discussing the event. He turned up the sound to an unbearably loud level.

"Sir?" Brenda asked.

"Fuck that," Brand said. "I need to watch my coverage. I think we're done here."

As soon as the room had cleared, he began searching through his briefcase, hoping to find a few stray miniature bottles of booze from the flight.

26 THE BIG EVENT

TOMMY WOKE TO DARKNESS and panic. He was fighting hard to breathe, but still felt like he couldn't get any air. He struggled to get up and get to the window, feeling dizzy and ready to pass out. He resorted to rolling off the bed, landing in an explosion of pain on the stained, flimsy carpet, face down in its stench. *I can't breathe. Fucking cancer must be in my lungs now.*

He tried to crawl toward the door, but after a few failed pushes realized he wasn't going to make it before he lost consciousness. *Think. Think, damn it. You can't fail now.* He felt for the St. Michael medallion from Moses. *Not yet. Can't die yet. Help me out, Moses.*

He turned onto his back, looking up at the nightstand. A cord hung from it, and he reached out and tried to pull it as everything slowly started to fade to black. He pulled again and saw the edge of the phone appear over the lip of the top of the nightstand. *Almost. Come on, damn it. Suck it up, Marine.*

One more pull, his chest heaving, his throat wheezing and gasping for air, and it came crashing down, just missing his head.

He grasped the receiver and brought it to his face, then laid it on the carpet. He reached out for the keypad, hearing the dial tone, afraid it would time out, and pressed the glowing button labeled Front Desk.

He heard a voice and responded with what he believed could be his last words. "Help me."

~*~

He came to, this time in blinding light instead of darkness. His vision was blurry, and he heard the static chatter of people talking on radios. They were moving around him, and he was off the floor, on a gurney. He was breathing.

A Latina woman in white leaned over him.

"Carmen?" he asked.

"Easy, sir," she said. "Is Carmen your wife? We couldn't find any emergency contact info in your things."

"Where am I? What's happening?" He looked up and the smoke-and-water stained ceiling answered the first question.

"You're in your motel room. You had some kind of attack and weren't breathing. We're the ambulance squad. Lucky for you, we got here just in time. We dosed you with albuterol to open up your lungs. Do you have asthma?"

"No, I don't," he said. "I think it was just a panic attack. I'm under a lot of stress lately. I have a lot of trouble sleeping, and I worry a lot. This toxic waste dump of a motel doesn't help the lungs, either."

A black EMT joined them. "We're going to take you to the hospital. They'll run some tests and get to the bottom of it."

"Nope," Tommy said. "No hospitals. No doctors. I'll be fine." He was still wheezing.

"Sir, it could come right back, as soon as the bronchodilator wears off. It probably will, in fact."

He again tried to summon a way out. "Alright, I lied. I do have asthma. I thought I was over it; I haven't had an attack in quite a while. I stupidly didn't pack my inhalers for my trip here. Can you give me a few to use until I reach my doc in the morning and have him call in a script?"

They reluctantly agreed and left. Tommy crawled shakily back into bed.

~*~

He woke again, wheezing. It was daylight. He reached over for the inhaler, hit on it hard, and began the slow, painful process of getting out of bed, getting to the bathroom, and taking his pills. He wasn't going to bother with a bath. *I'll likely be dead or in jail by the end of the day. Fuck it.*

After wheeling himself to the closet, he sat for a moment and looked at the uniform hanging there. *U.S. Marine Corps dress blues. Finest uniform in the world.* He took some time to think back over his years of service: his pride at completing the rigorous basic training, going home in that same blue dress uniform to his proud mother, then shipping off to Vietnam. Then the lifetime he seemed to spend there, and finally coming home in his dress blues to start a new life.

Life is so long, but goes by so quickly. I wish I would've cherished every day. Here I am, at the end of it, not knowing what comes after it. I don't really care, though, as long as I can be with my boy. All I want before I go is to take this scum out so he can't change this world for the worse, and to kiss Tara one more time.

The thoughts gave him energy, and he determinedly pulled the uniform down and dressed. He wheeled over to the smudged, cloudy full-length mirror on the bathroom door and applied his ribbons and medals. *The Corps was good for me. Taught me discipline. I'll need it today. One last combat mission.*

He made his way outside. TQ helped him into the van and handed him a cup of coffee. "Damn, looking sharp today, Marine!" TQ exclaimed.

Tommy took a long slug of the coffee. "You're a savior, TQ, thanks," Tommy said.

"You heading to the gig this early?"

"Right. I like to be early, get a good spot, find my way around."

"You don't sound too good today, my friend," TQ said.

"Yeah, must be the humidity here screwing up my asthma," Tommy said. "Sorry I can't talk much."

They rode in silence. Tommy watched out of the van windows as laborers labored, people who were probably illegal working and perspiring in the heat. He thought of how they were paying taxes for the benefit of others, to pay for things like social security that they would never be able to take advantage of as noncitizens.

People of all working classes rushed down crowded sidewalks, looking stressed and unhappy. *For what? To put up with this and get a few weeks a year off the treadmill? We're just like disposable batteries, cogs in a wheel. This is your one life. Treasure every day. Nobody ever died wishing they had worked more.*

He knew they had no choice, and that they were likely doing what they were doing for their children's sake.

A limo pulled up next to them at a red light. Tommy peered inside and saw a well-dressed man and woman sitting in the back, enjoying drinks and laughing.

"Probably some of Brand's people right there," TQ said. "Probably going to the event tonight the same way, in style and on the taxpayer's dime. I can't change it, so I ain't worrying about it."

"Either that," Tommy responded, "or they're executives hoarding the profits while screwing over the people that work for them." He looked back over at the limo. *I wish I had more time, so I could take some of you greedy fuckers out, too.*

He tried to block out the pain and effort that every breath was starting to take. Pulling the inhaler from his pocket, he took a puff of it. He considered taking more of the pain meds, too, but didn't want to make himself drowsy or dull his mind further.

They approached the convention center. Tommy removed the bracelet Micco had given him and reversed it, so the arrow pointed to the right. *Time for war.* He placed his hand over his dress jacket and felt the St. Michael medallion from Moses and the peace sign necklace from Tara. *I have all my talismans. Be with me, all of you.*

"Looks like all the entrances are still blocked off," TQ informed him.

"Go around to the employee entrance," Tommy advised.

TQ unloaded him, and he proceeded to the door. It opened, and the same security guard stepped out to hold it for him.

"Back again?" the guard asked. "You look great, sir. Not too many people around yet, it's very early."

"I guess I'm too excited to sit at home," Tommy said. "I want to be able to take it all in before it gets too crazy. Hey, that same driver will pick me up later. Can you make sure he'll be able to get through?"

The guard went over to TQ and Tommy entered the building. He took in the fully assembled stage from the concourse, stopping to pull his event instruction sheet from the tiller bag and pick out approximately where he would be located. He took note of the entrance that led from their holding room to the stage as well.

He went back down the elevator to the ground floor, passing the growing number of workers scuttling about making last-minute preparations. He found his way to the box office area and wheeled himself outside. After some time, he discovered the cordoned-off areas where the protesters and supporters outside would be located.

He spent time rolling around among the workers and security people, chatting them up, making himself known to them. He cruised along the concrete jersey barriers, looking for one with just the kind of defect he needed to place his small package.

As he was making his way back toward the building, a gruff supervisor called him out. "What are you doing out here?"

"Easy, pal. I used to be in construction. Just checking out how everything works. Killing time until I have to be inside. I got to piss, headed there now."

The man continued to stare until Tommy entered the building.

He made his way to the backstage hallway that led to the holding room and green room. People were starting to come in waves now, as the hour of the event grew nearer. The hallways were becoming clogged with people going in each direction, their badges flapping around on the lanyards around their necks.

His breathing became more labored, and his chest tightened as he pushed himself toward his goal—the green room just ahead. *I just have to get the gun out of that toilet and back in my bag, and I'm all set.*

As he made his final approach, he saw Gloria exit the green room, locking it on the way out. *Shit.*

"Hey, Gloria," he called to her cheerfully. "Remember me? Listen, I gotta go again, and this one's a lot easier to use with the wheelchair and all..."

She cut him off. "Yes, of course, I remember you. You look fantastic! You look ready to step right back on the battlefield. I'm so happy our vets are coming for the event this evening."

"Thanks, thanks. Yeah, I'm still kind of sick, do you think..."

"Oh, no. I'm sorry, sir. The room is sealed off now until the security teams come through to search it before Mr. Brand arrives. Nobody goes in until they do that, and then after that nobody goes in except Mr. Brand, his family, and closest advisers."

Shit. Shit, shit, shit.

"Let me help you to the holding room bathroom, though. Let's hurry, we don't want a mess," Gloria said musically, positioning herself behind him.

She pushed Tommy into the holding room. Several other vets were already there, sitting together and having loud, animated conversations. She pushed him past them and directly to the men's room.

"I'm gonna leave you off here, sir. Do you need help? I can ask one of the other fellows out there."

"No, this is fine, thanks," Tommy said.

He went into the handicapped stall and considered his situation. *Something will break. Don't panic. I'll figure out a way to get in there.* He rolled out of the stall and looked at himself in the mirror. *I look like I'm a hundred years old. I feel even older. But I'm wearing this uniform, and I have a job to do for my country. I've had karma with me all along. I'm meant to do this.*

He hit on the inhaler and injected his last shot of the steroids, then rolled back into the holding room. The others there greeted him, and he joined them for their stories and recollections. They were all old, like him. He was growing more fatigued, and nausea was creeping in as time passed.

As the start time drew nearer, he heard a commotion in the hallway, and the door burst open. Security people came through, pushing someone who was hunched down in the middle of them. They closed the door behind them. The man in the middle stood up, clearly shaken. *Brand.*

One of the officers addressed them. "Sorry for the commotion. We discovered a security breach next door. The room is being cleared, and the venue is being scanned again. It's going to take a while, so we can't allow anyone to enter or leave this room during that time. The good news is that Mr. Brand will be able to spend extra time with you before you all go out on stage."

Tommy realized they had found the gun, and more panic set in. His heart raced. *There goes my plan B.*

His mind no longer quickly found solutions to problems, but he pushed it relentlessly. His backup plan had been flawed, and he cursed himself for not having a more solid one. *I should have had a solid plan B and a plan C. Some fucking cop I am. Stupid.*

He had noticed a few of Brand's people had entered at the back of the pack that had come through the door, including the woman he'd met at the campaign offices. *Brenda, I think it was.*

Another woman, whom he assumed was the publicist, was taking advantage of the opportunity to photograph Brand with some of the vets. A pool reporter and cameraman were shooting footage of it all. The reporter was excitedly telling her audience about the dramatic events. Brand had recovered and was now happily soaking up the attention.

He caught Brenda's eye and motioned to her.

"Mr. Domingo, happy to see you here," she greeted him.

"Hi, I hope everything is okay. This is all a bit intimidating. What happened?"

"They found a gun next door. No idea how long it's been there, but we have to assume it has something to do with the event. You're safe though. That's why we do these searches. The security team is quite thorough."

"Geez. What the hell is wrong with people these days?" Tommy said. "I'd like to meet Mr. Brand, but I can't get in the middle of all that chaos over there. I have PTSD and some kind of crowd phobia."

"Don't worry, I'll handle that for you, Mr. Domingo. Just give me a little time to let him get through the rest of the group, and I'll set it up."

He waited, watching the candidate with hatred. Now that he was in the same room, he despised the man even more. Brand's every gesture was pretentious, and he reeked of narcissism and entitlement.

Finally, as Brand had made his rounds, Tommy saw Brenda take him by the arm and say something to him. He glanced Tommy's way, and they both started over. It was a surreal moment for Tommy. *I wish I had the damn gun right now, to get this over with.*

"Mr. Brand, this is Mr. Domingo. He's got a Bronze Star and Purple Heart, as you can see."

Brand squinted at the medals on Tommy's chest.

He's too vain to wear the glasses he needs in public.

Brand took Tommy's outstretched hand in a weak, limp shake and mumbled something about his service to the country. Tommy noticed that up close, without all of the makeup, the blood vessels in his face and nose were burst. His skin was clammy, he was sweating, and appeared to be shaking slightly. *Damn, he is a drunk. He's got it bad. He needs a drink, just as I hoped.*

Brand turned back to Brenda excitedly. "Hey, this one's in a wheelchair. Let's make sure he's up front on the stage, and right next to me. Go tell Stinson to rearrange the seating chart, hurry."

She moved off, and Tommy took advantage of the opportunity. He pulled on Brand's sleeve and motioned for him to lean down.

"Listen," Tommy whispered. "I hate to admit it, but I'm a bit of a drunk, and I need a drink to be able to get out there in front of all those people. And, I brought you some excellent bourbon, but your staff wouldn't take it—something about regulations. Do you think we could sneak over to your private room next door? It's got to be secure by now. There's nobody in there."

Brand took the bait. He motioned to a member of the security detail, who came over immediately. "I've got a better idea," he said excitedly to Tommy.

"Have you guys finished clearing this bathroom?" Brand asked the guard. "You fuck-wads almost got me killed by not being thorough next door."

"It's clear, sir. It's been checked twice. We've escorted everyone who needed to go down the hall to the public restroom. We're holding the one in here just for you, and you alone."

"Good," Brand said. He noticed the news crew filming them and raised his voice, making it deeper. "This man needs to go to the restroom, and I won't have him sent out into the hall to the public bathroom. I'm going to take care of him myself."

He went behind Tommy and pushed him toward the men's room. The security lead and camera crew followed.

Brand pushed the door open and ordered the guard and news team to stay outside as the camera rolled. "Let this veteran have his dignity."

When they were inside with the door closed Brand quickly turned to him. "What've you got?"

Tommy separated his legs and rummaged in the tiller bag behind them. He pulled out a silver flask, and then a paper bag with a bottle inside. He unscrewed the cap of his flask and pretended to take a swallow, placing his tongue against the opening. "I drink the cheap stuff."

He raised it to Brand, who grimaced. "Christ, I can't drink from that after you just did," Brand said. "What else you got?" He motioned at the bag.

"Mr. Brand, I'm a huge supporter. I spent my whole disability check on this when I heard it was available, as thanks for what you're doing for our country."

Brand grabbed the bag and slid the bottle out. "Sweet Jesus, Martin Mills. I've heard about this stuff."

Without so much as a thank you, he opened it hastily and took a long drink. "We gotta get out of here before they come in to check on me," he said. He hit it again, then replaced the cap, put the bottle back in the bag, and went to the door. "Come in here," he said to the guard.

The man entered, and Brand pushed the bag into his hand. "Don't let anyone see this, but keep it handy."

Brand went to the sink and scooped up handfuls of water to rinse out his breath, then pulled a tin of mints from his jacket pocket, shook a few out, and placed them in his mouth. "Bring this guy out after he has a chance to take a piss," he told the guard as he went through the door.

~*~

Tommy suffered through the event, and thankfully it went quickly. His breathing became more labored each hour, the inhaler providing less benefit each time it was employed. As soon as it was over and they were back in the holding room, he saw Brand pull the guard back into the men's room. He discretely called TQ and began to let himself out when he ran into Brenda.

"Mr. Domingo, let me bring you to the reception. Mr. Brand will be sitting at a table with all of you vets. I hear the food will be delicious."

"No thanks," Tommy wheezed. "I'm not feeling well, and I'm overstimulated from all this. I've had a wonderful day, and I'd like to be on my way. I need to get home to my meds and my dog."

"I'm going to have one of the security people escort you out. There's complete mayhem outside the building, and it's becoming dangerous. Do you have a ride?"

"Yeah," Tommy said. "I have one of those handicapped vans. I set it up with security; he'll be waiting for me."

After TQ had loaded him, they passed by the mayhem going on outside the building. Tommy could hear the groups yelling at each other, chanting, screaming. He saw the banners of the Brand Brigade, and the pennants of the protesters raised high. The police were trying to disperse them and send everyone on their way.

"It's fucking crazy what we're coming to, isn't it, TQ?" he asked in a whisper. "Damn scary."

"Scarier still if you're a black guy," TQ responded.

Tommy noticed flickering ambulance and police lights deep into the crowd. "Looks like someone got hurt."

"It was on the radio just before you came out. They don't know what the hell happened, but witnesses said some dude in that Brand Brigade was talking on his phone and the damn thing blew up. Took his head and arm right off."

"Jesus," Tommy said, smiling. "I'm sure glad it was on that side and not the protesters." He tried to suppress a laugh, and it launched him into a fit of coughs and hacks. He worked desperately between them to pull in air. His body felt stuffed as if a full meal were through every part of it. *I'm loaded up good with it now, this fucking disease.*

"You ain't sounding so well, Tommy. You want to head to the ER?"

"No, to the hotel," Tommy answered carefully, trying not to kick off another fit. "I need to pick up my stuff, then I have some other places I'd like you to take me to. You busy tonight?"

"Same as always—not so much. Handicapped folks are all sleeping by now."

"Good, take yourself off the clock if you can. I'll make it worth your while."

They pulled up to the motel. Tommy had TQ help him retrieve his already-packed sea bag from against the wall and put it in the van. He went to use the bathroom, and as he entered and closed the door, he noticed the two empty black vials floating in the toilet. *Jesus, they didn't flush.*

He pulled them out and filled them with water from the sink, then finished his business and flushed them again, this time making sure they didn't return to the surface.

On the way out of the room, he paused to look in one last time. *I wonder if they'll make a museum out of it, like that school book depository in Dallas.*

"Alright, TQ, swing by that Army/Navy store if you can. I left something in there. Hopefully it's still open."

As they took the exit and started down the boulevard that the shop was on, Tommy discreetly pulled out his cell phone. He held it low so that TQ wouldn't see the glow of the lights.

"Looks like they're closed," TQ said as they drove by.

"Damn. Alright, get back on the highway and head south then." As they crested a hill on the on-ramp, Tommy entered 666 on the phone key-pad and pressed the 'Send' button. He glanced back over his shoulder in the direction of the store and saw a satisfying burst of orange-and-red light.

A muffled pop followed it. The sound reminded him of the last kernel of popcorn bursting as he stood vigilantly at the microwave before watching a movie with Bobby.

"Where to?" TQ said, his attention on the highway ahead.

"Islamorada," Tommy responded.

"Huh? Did you say Islamorada?"

"Damn right. Here's five hundred bucks. Keep it quiet as long as you can, TQ. They'll come around, eventually. Just tell them you took some crazy old guy to Islamorada and you were well paid. That's all you know."

"What the hell did you do, Tommy?"

"I made the world a better place tonight. And that's all I want to say about it. I'm gonna try to sleep a bit now, TQ. Thank you for all you've done for me."

TARA LAY BACK ON HER BED after a long, exhausting day. The market had been busy, and it had helped the day pass quickly. She still eagerly waited for some sign that Tommy was coming back. Whitey leaped up to join her, nuzzling her arm until she began petting him.

She thought back to the blissful days they had spent on the private key and wished every day could be like that. *In paradise, with someone I love.* Life had never worked out that way for her. *I never found someone right, until him. He was my last shot to not die alone.*

She realized she was hoping for something that was highly unlikely—that he would somehow beat the disease and they might live happily ever after. "Such is my lot in life, Whitey."

Unable to sleep, she picked up the remote and switched on the TV. A reality show featuring people in the wilderness was playing, and she watched as they schemed and stabbed each other in the back. *Is this what we've come to as a society? Smarter savages?*

She fell asleep until Whitey became restless, waking her. After she went to use the bathroom and got back into bed, she noticed the dog observing the screen. The news was on, and they were showing candidate Brand with some veterans at an event in Miami.

Then she saw him, barely recognizable, sitting in a wheelchair while Brand talked to him and then began wheeling him somewhere. "Oh my God, Whitey. What the hell is he up to?" *I think I know.*

Everything changed at that moment. Tara thought back to Tommy's words, what she knew he'd done before, and what little time he had left.

She began to worry about him, and then for herself. She fought with her conscience, which was telling her to make a call, to perhaps save a life. And then she thought about the lives that could be lost in many ways if that horrible man were to be elected, the many people who'd suffer, and what it would mean for the country, if not the world. *For my daughter, and her kids, and theirs.*

~*~

It was very late, and Brenda wanted badly to go home. She tried to make sense of what Brand was saying to her. His voice was thick and slurred, and he leaned back into the plush leather chair in frustration. She looked over at Carenton.

"What the hell have you guys been doing?" she asked. "He handles his booze pretty well. I've seen him knock down a bottle of bourbon before and it hardly fazed him."

Carenton shrugged his shoulders. "Maybe because we made him wait all day? He's used to a steady stream of the stuff. Maybe he guzzled it, and it hit him too hard."

"Doesn't sound plausible," Brenda said. "What was he drinking?"

"Some rare stuff," Carenton responded. "He would only give me a shot—said he had to cherish it—then he polished the whole damn bottle off over the course of the night."

"Rare stuff...where did he get it?"

"He said one of the vets gave it to him as a gift. The guy in the wheelchair, with the white beard."

She looked over at Brand, who was now slumped over, asleep on the couch. The pieces clicked in her mind. "Jesus. Where's the bottle?"

"Over there, in the trash."

She hurried across the room and retrieved it from the waste basket. *Martin Mills—the same bottle.* She ran to the desk, picked up the phone, and dialed 911. "I need an ambulance, quick. And the police. Please hurry."

~*~

Catherine Brand looked down at her husband in his hospital bed. *Stupid fucking drunk. Whoever did this to you did me a real favor.* When the nurses and others were present, she went through the motions that a grieving, worried wife would; holding his hand, talking to him, asking him to come back to her.

He stirred occasionally.

The doctor entered the room. "What's happening to my husband?" she asked. "Why is he like this, with all these tubes in his arms and nose?"

"We're trying to figure it out, Mrs. Brand," the doctor answered. "We believe he's been poisoned, but we don't have complete toxicology reports yet. The team is having a hard time identifying what he was given. It was something in the bourbon he drank last night. That's all we know right now. We're testing the bottle as well."

The doctor took some vitals and observed him for a few moments, then left.

She got up and looked out the window, at the media trucks outside and the gathered crowds in the morning light.

Taking her seat next to him, she began to think about what this meant for her. *If he dies, I'm free. I can start over. I'll choose someone for love this time, not ambition. I've learned my lesson. I don't give a damn if he's penniless, I'll find someone that will make me happy.* She grew excited at the prospect, and looked at the tubes, wondering if she could help things along by pinching any of them closed.

She thought she heard him make a noise, and leaned in close to his mouth.

"What, honey? What did you say? I'm here, honey. Speak up."

"Mommy," she heard him whisper.

She looked and saw that his eyes were open for the first time since she'd arrived. She leaned in close again, this time next to his ear. "Fuck you, buddy," she said.

His eyes closed, and he became silent and still. Catherine went back to her romance novel, occasionally glancing up at the coverage on the television.

Suddenly he began to convulse. She looked at the equipment, the numbers and graph lines jumping erratically. Then, all at once, his convulsions stopped, the heartbeat graph flat-lined, and the machines began to sing their alerts in harmony.

She put the novel down and began her performance.

28 ALREADY GONE

WHITEY SEEMED UNUSUALLY excited and restless throughout the night. He had slept with Tara every night on the bed, while Ol' Jerry laid next to them on the floor. She hadn't slept well either. She knew it wasn't just because of the dog—it was because she had seen Tommy at the rally, amid the chaos, and now there had been a murder and firebombing nearby, according to the late news last night.

It was earlier than she usually got started, and still dark. She rallied herself to get up and shower. *The market is always waiting.* She turned on the television with apprehension and began to get dressed.

The news anchors were discussing the horrible events from the previous night, and how they had tainted the positive publicity that Brand had hoped to gain from the event. They showed video of him again, in the room with the veterans, wheeling Tommy in a wheelchair. It saddened her. *Is Tommy really that far gone already?* She wondered why Brand wasn't already dead, now having guessed what Tommy was up to.

Whitey watched the screen from the bed, having moved over to lay on her pillow. He jumped up and barked once, then circled around on the bed, whining, before burying his head in the coverings.

The anchors continued to discuss Brand.

"...the candidate has reportedly been overcome with stress and compassion due to one of his supporters being murdered in such a grisly fashion, and has canceled his events for the day. The police are looking into whether the killing and the firebombing of a nearby Army/Navy store are related, as the explosives used in both are reportedly similar. A fake bomb was also found, fashioned to blend in with the concrete dividers in the crowd."

The pieces began to fall together in her mind as she finished getting ready for work. She turned off the television and locked up as she left, the two dogs in tow. She placed Whitey in the basket on her handlebars and headed down the road to the farmer's market with Ol' Jerry trotting beside her.

Whitey became more restless as Tara neared their destination, standing in the basket with his front paws on the edge. "Stay, Whitey. Stay," she commanded. As she came within view of her stall, the dog leaped from the basket and ran, disappearing under the canvas fronting.

She pulled up on the bike and approached cautiously, afraid that the investigators had come back. She unlocked the padlocks at the bottom of the canvas fronting and pulled it up carefully, as it was still too dark to see clearly. *Only fruit and vegetables. Where's Whitey?*

She crept in cautiously, noticing the door to the back office was ajar. Whitey was whimpering from behind it. She pushed it open, and he was there, unconscious and breathing in a heavy, gurgling rattle, sitting in the wheelchair. Whitey had jumped up onto his lap. He was dressed in his Marine Corps uniform, but his jacket and shirt were unbuttoned, exposing the peace medallion she had given him, a religious medallion, and his dog tags.

"Tommy!" she exclaimed, running to him. She shook him and patted his cheek.

He came to slowly, and feebly motioned to the floor. "Inhaler," he said, almost inaudibly.

She turned and saw it, then grabbed it and placed it in his mouth, pumping it vigorously.

She paused to gauge the effect. His breathing was slightly better, but he was clearly in bad shape. She ran back out to pull down the canvas stall in front and lash it into place.

"Honey, I'm home. I'm back, like I promised," he wheezed, smiling slightly at her.

"Oh, Tommy. I love you. I'm going to call an ambulance..."

"No. Too late. Please. Let's go to our place. I just want to be there, with you. There's not much time. Cops will come, and I'm almost finished. I feel it, coming for me now, Tara."

She leaned in and hugged him, then kissed him. "Wait here. I'm going to go get Micco's truck. I won't say why. I'll take you out through the back."

She rushed out and pulled the vehicle to the rear loading area of her stall. She jumped out, leaving it running, and came around to open the passenger door. Back in the office, she pushed Tommy's wheelchair out into the bright sunlight, up to the open door. Whitey circled them, barking, clearly not understanding what was happening.

Tommy tried to rise to get in, and she had to help him. *He's lost so much weight—like he hasn't eaten at all since he left.* She was able to get him to the seat, and he immediately lay down across it. She collapsed the wheelchair and removed some blankets from the truck bed before placing it in.

She covered him, and he said that he loved her again. Whitey jumped into the back as she went into retrieve Ol' Jerry, and then pulled the truck away from the market.

"Hang in there, Tommy, we're on the way."

She resisted the urge to speed, not wanting to attract attention. She took the back roads, stopping at every stop sign for the minimum time before surging forward. Whitey continued to whine, and she could hear Tommy's horrific rattle as he struggled to breathe.

Finally, she came to the narrow bridge that crossed over to the private key they had spent their amazing days on. "Almost there," she said, now crying. "Hold on, Tommy."

She pulled up to the bungalow and retrieved the wheelchair. As she loaded him into it, he told her again that he loved her.

She got him inside and went to the bedroom. "Come on, Tommy, let's get you up on the bed." This time the effort to move him was mostly hers. When he was completely on the bed, his upper body propped up with pillows, she used the inhaler again, to try to dilate his lungs enough for him to talk. He motioned to her to keep pumping, and she did until it ran out.

Whitey begged to be lifted up and join him and Tara did so. The dog nestled himself against Tommy and whimpered. Tommy placed his hand under his shirt again, over the two medallions and the dog tags.

She got up and turned on the radio, tuning to the local-easy listening station for some soothing music. A jazz version of "Stormy Monday" was playing, and it seemed to bring a slight smile to Tommy's face.

She lay next to him, and they faced each other, professing their love again and again as they both cried and the sun continued to rise over the ocean through the panoramic bedroom window.

The radio personality interrupted the music.

"In important breaking news, Thomas Brand, Republican candidate for President of the United States, has died. The only information we have—and this is an unverified rumor—is that he reportedly lapsed into a coma after an exhausting day yesterday, which was followed by a night of heavy drinking."

She looked at Tommy, and he smiled. "The world's a better place now, Tara."

"Tommy, did you..."

"Don't," he whispered between rattling, heaving breaths. "You don't know anything, Tara. You can't. Plausible deniability, remember?"

Whitey lay at his side, silent, his unwavering gaze trained on his master. Tommy had his hand on the dog's back, and he seemed to be trying to soothe him. She put her hands on his chest lightly, wishing she could heal him. Then she leaned in and kissed him.

"That's...all I wanted...one last kiss from you. And...to die heroically...not pathetic..."

"Just Tommy, you're my hero. You're many people's hero now," she said through her growing hysteria.

He turned his head slightly, to the huge orange ball of the sun, now fully up over the ocean and casting the room in a brilliant, heavenly glow. "What a beautiful...place to die. In heaven...with an angel by my side. You...gave me love...peace, Tara. It was beautiful...like you. I'll see you there...someday. You...and me..."

She frantically tried the spent inhaler again as he closed his eyes. His breaths were coming more slowly now, the rattling louder each time, sounding like a wasted attempt to suck an empty drink through a straw.

She thought she heard him say something else between the ragged breaths. She leaned in close, hoping he would repeat it. "Going home, Whitey. Wait here, boy.

He struggled to inhale and continued. "Hello, Bobby. Hi, Moses. Hey, Sensei. I'm here..." she thought she heard him say. She considered whether it was cancer in his brain, causing delusions. Or perhaps he was already partly in another world, one beyond theirs. *Maybe he's with angels there to greet him.*

She took his hand and put her head back down on his chest, listening to the last beats of his heart growing fainter, and the struggling of his tortured lungs, until he was gone. His firm grip on her hand relaxed, and she stayed there, lying quietly beside him with the dog until she had cried herself to sleep. She knew it wouldn't be long before they tracked him to this place.

~*~

She woke when Whitey barked sharply and jumped from the bed, startling her. She heard faint activity outside and saw a shadow move in the window. As she watched the bedroom doorknob, she saw it move slightly while Whitey stood in front of the door, barking.

The door burst open, and several men in black tactical gear flooded in, shouting "FBI, don't move!"

They formed a semi-circle around the bed, each in a rigid stance, pointing weapons at her and Tommy. "Relax," she said, crying, running her fingers through his short, patchy silver hair. "He's already gone. He's in a far better place."

"Step away, ma'am," one of them said to her.

She leaned over, kissed him on the forehead, and complied. They placed her in handcuffs, and as they led her outside, she heard them reporting their status and asking the ambulance to proceed down the road to them.

She sat in the rear of a police vehicle, watching through her tears as a light summer rain shower streaked the windows of the car. They pulled the gurney from the bungalow, the depleted form of her lover strapped down under a brilliant white sheet. They loaded it into the ambulance, with what seemed like reverence.

The shower cleared as suddenly as it had appeared, and the sun once again illuminated the ocean and beach beyond the small house they had shared for one perfect week together.

"Goodbye, Just Tommy," she said, as it swallowed him up and they closed the doors behind him.

29 HONEYMOONERS

WHITEY LAY ON TARA'S LAP in the shade of the market stall. Most of the woven baskets were empty, and Tara stared off to the horizon beyond them.

Micco appeared in her field of vision, and she motioned to the empty chair beside her.

"How're you holding up, Tara?" he asked.

"It's a process," she responded. "I'll be okay. I probably shouldn't be here, but it was unbearable sitting at home and hiding from the media. At least they've finally lost interest in me, for the most part. I just miss him, terribly."

"Me too. He's been an inspiration to me. I'm gonna get a new boat and name it after him."

"How did your questioning go, Micco? Are they charging you with anything?"

"No, they got nothing on me. I guess they're going with the lone wolf thing and don't want to bother. To tell you the truth, I think most of them view Tommy as a hero."

"Same here. I guess we go back to our old lives now."

"I'm looking forward to it, Tara. I'm going to head back down the row. Stop by and visit in a little while, okay?"

"Sure thing, kid," she responded.

She leaned back in the chair and stretched her legs out in front of her. Whitey shifted position and went back to his nap. As was her habit now, she replayed the first day she met Tommy, the first time they made love in his cabin, and their week at the private key, until she fell asleep.

She woke to a rumbling sound in the distance. Whitey perked up at the same time, and leaped from her lap. The dog ran to the edge of the road and looked down it in anticipation. He stood up on his hind legs, raising his two front feet and moving them in a rowing motion, as he did when he anxiously waited to be fed.

Tara got up and joined him, looking down the road to see what had gotten the dog's attention.

Through the shimmer of the heat on the blacktop, she saw a large touring motorcycle appear with two riders on board. A large American flag flapped from the top case on the back.

As it neared, she heard the Marvin Gaye hit "Mercy, Mercy Me" blaring through its sound system. The bike pulled into the market's parking lot. The driver shut down the engine, and both riders dismounted. They wore black leather vests with rocker patches emblazoned with 'Black Eagles MC' in gold lettering. Whitey circled them, barking excitedly.

The two removed their helmets, and the man and woman approached Tara. The man reached down and picked Whitey up, and the dog nuzzled in his arms.

"You must be Ms. Tara," the man said to her. "I'm Lukas Taylor, and this is my new wife, Tass. We're friends of Tommy Borata. We're on the way down through the Keys on our honeymoon, and we wanted to stop by to say hello."

Tara embraced them both, fighting back the tears again. "Yes, I'm Tara. I'm sorry I couldn't come up for the funeral. As you can guess, for a long time it was a circus around here with the media. I'm sure it was worse up there for all of you. Besides, I'm not much for funerals or good-byes. It's a hippie thing."

They laughed at the comment. Tara brought them into the stall, and they spent time reminiscing and telling Tommy stories. She carved a selection of fresh melons and served them on a platter, and made sandwiches for lunch. Micco joined them after a while and added his own sea-faring tale as the group sat mesmerized by the close call with the Coast Guard and Tommy's quick thinking and bravery.

"Amazing how a man can endure all that while he's dying of cancer," Lukas mused.

"He was no ordinary man," Tara added. "It was the Marine in him. He never quit."

There was a moment of silence, and she sensed they wanted to move on, but that there was something else to their visit.

"So, Tara," Tass began carefully. "We have a few things for you. You don't have to take them—if not, we understand."

"Bring it on, and let's see," she said.

Lukas reached into his vest, pulled out a funeral memorial card, and handed it to Tara.

She examined it lovingly and smiled. "That's my Tommy. Thank you for remembering to bring one to me." She kissed it and held it out to examine his picture on it again.

Whitey continued to share time between Tara, Lukas, and Tass. "Tommy told me that Whitey had belonged to your Uncle Moses, and to you for a while, Lukas," Tara said. "Do you want to bring him home?"

"If he's happy here, we'd like to leave him with you, Tara. But if he's too much…"

"Oh, thank God," she interrupted. "I love this dog. He's a little bit of Tommy here with me. I promised Tommy I'd look after Whitey. My own dog passed away just recently, on top of everything else. I don't think Ol' Jerry could stand to see me so sad every day. Whitey is all I have left."

"This was Tommy's final place, and Whitey seems happy here with you," Tass added.

"I don't know what I'd do without him," Tara said.

"Sure thing, then," Lukas said. "There's something else before we have to go, though."

He got up and went to the motorcycle, unfastening one of the saddlebags. He pulled a wooden box from it and presented it to Tara.

She looked down at it on her lap, in shock. It was engraved with 'Thomas Borata,' an Eagle, Globe, and Anchor Marine Corps logo, an image of St. Michael, and a peace sign.

"It's Tommy," Tass said gently. "He asked us to do this, but to tell you that you don't have to…"

Tara burst into tears, hugging the box to her breast. "He always comes back to me, like he said he would. We talked about cremation, and I think he gave me a sense of what he wanted."

With that, they stood and said their goodbyes. Tara and Micco watched the couple ride down the road, the music resuming as they waved and disappeared into the distance.

~*~

"You ready?" Micco asked Tara.

"Ready as ever. Let's do this."

They walked to the shoreline and placed their bags into a dugout canoe with outriggers on both sides. The sides were painted with bright

Seminole glyphs, and under the back lip in red letters read 'Domingo.' Micco and Tara pulled it into the light surf and hopped on board. They paddled quickly to move beyond the surf line, and then slowed their pace to catch their breath.

"I never thought this old pet project of mine would have such a reverent purpose," Micco said.

"It all comes back to karma," Tara responded. "I think everything has a purpose, and you were guided to this one, Micco. Tommy would absolutely love this."

She opened her bag, produced the box and sat it next to her. "I saved just a little of him to keep with me always," she said.

Micco looked at her, confused, and she patted a silver teardrop pendant that hung from her neck.

They moved out further, waiting as the tide provided a lull in the sea. Micco used his paddle to spin the boat to face a bungalow in the distance, sitting on a small private key.

Tara pulled the box onto her lap and kissed it. She then lifted the box over her head.

"Be well on your journey, Tommy," Micco said solemnly.

"Goodbye again, Just Tommy. You were the one I'd always searched for. Our time together was short, but perfect. I'll always love you, and I'll see you when my time here is finished as well."

She opened the box and tipped it slightly forward. The ocean breeze seemed to pick up on command, and the contents of the wooden box were swept out slowly, curling into the wind and then scattering until they were no longer visible.

When it was empty, she closed it and placed it again by her side. They wordlessly paddled back to shore, the sun setting in a large orange glow on the horizon behind them.

EPILOGUE/LETTERS

Nurse Carmen,

By now you know the news. I wanted to thank you for caring for me and tolerating my nonsense. You got this old Marine through some pretty tough times. I'm sure Moses would say the same. In fact, by the time you read this, he'll be right here next to me, and he says hello. The dynamic duo will be together again. Hopefully in a place that's heavenly and not hell.

I had a lot of insurance—it was supposed to be for my boy. When he passed, I sat down and tried to think of the people that make a difference for others. Those are the kind I want to help. People like you.

I remember you telling me the story about the Barbie camper you had wanted so badly for Christmas, and that you still had it, much worse for wear and tear.

I took the liberty of purchasing a new one for you, which you should find outside the hospital on the day you receive this letter. A beautiful, shiny camper van of your own. Find someone nice, as nice as you, and take it and explore this beautiful country. Don't work so hard!

I also established a fund for you to continue your education and become a doctor, as you wanted to. The amount there should be plenty to live on until you complete your studies. You are a natural caregiver. Please take advantage of this and go on helping the sick. Make me proud and find a cure for this horrible disease.

Love, Tommy

Lukas,

I know that all your Uncle Moses wanted was the best for you. The Black Eagles bailed me out of a jam and may have saved my life that day at the cemetery. For that, I owe you. On the day you receive this, you should find a set of brand-new bikes parked outside the apartments. The Eagles will now fly in style, which means less time fixing the bikes, and more time riding.

I also left you and Tass a nice sum of money to begin your new lives together. Congratulations if you're already married by the time you receive this, and sorry I haven't been able to keep in touch.

Stay true to your oath to be a force for goodness. We don't have enough of that in this world.

Love, Tommy

Margie,

I'm sorry I had to go in the direction I did. After our son's death, I was empty, and all I could look forward to was being with him. Hopefully, that's where I am as you read this letter. We had so many wonderful years together, Margie, and I want you to know that you will always be a part of me, even where I am now.

If you can do anything for Bobby and me, you know what it is. Put the bottle away and be as healthy and happy as you can. We'll be cheering you on—just look skyward if you ever need encouragement.

Love, Tommy

Dearest Tara,

As you read this, it's over, and hopefully I died in your arms. It's all I wanted. You gave me the most beautiful days and nights of my life. You are a beautiful soul, and if the entire world were made in your image, we'd have no hatred.

It was excruciating to leave you after our little vacation, especially after those beautiful days we had together on the private key. But I had to do what I did, for reasons you are well aware of now. When I discovered that I was sick and my time was limited, I decided to leave the world a better place than I found it. I think I've done that.

Please care for Whitey as I would. I left you a sum of money for him and for yourself, in case you want to give up the fruits and veggies business someday. Love him and apologize to him for me. I hope we can have dogs in heaven. If so, I look forward very much to the three of us reuniting someday.

Hopefully, I got that one last kiss. I left instructions to Lukas to bring me back to you one more time. I hope that was alright, and I trust that you will know what to do.

Love eternally,

Just Tommy

The End

If you enjoyed this book, please leave a brief review on Amazon or Goodreads. Thanks!

Sign up for the newsletter at billydecarlo.com to stay informed about progress and release dates for new books, audiobooks, and other news.

Order the boxed set or other books in this trilogy: https://www.amazon.com/gp/product/B073ZLK3T S/ref=series_rw_dp_sw

Vigilante Angels Book I: The Priest

Vigilante Angels Book II: The Cop

Billy DeCarlo

Billy DeCarlo is an American author of novels and short stories.

A Note to My Readers

At my core, I'm just a humble, blue-collar guy who has always loved to write. To be honest, I don't seek fame; perhaps just enough fortune to pay the bills. I write because I need to write.

The most rewarding thing a writer can receive is a review on Amazon and/or Goodreads from those who enjoyed the work.

The most constructive thing a writer can receive is a private message with anything that can help to improve his or her work.

The advice to writers about marketing their books is consistent in stating that a writer 'platform' is necessary for any writer to be successful.

As someone who would rather spend time writing than maintaining a plethora of social media sites, and to whom privacy is a very important consideration, I hope you will understand and view my work based on its content, not my social skills. I do hope that you sign up for the newsletter at my website so that you hear about future books, editions, and news.

Reviews are the currency of the craft. If you enjoyed my book, please take time to write a review. If you didn't, please send me a private message via one of the below means. Inquiries will be fielded by my wonderful wife, who is my publicist. Thank you for your understanding, and I hope you enjoyed this book!

billydecarlo.com

facebook.com/BillyDeCarloAuthor

twitter.com/BillyDeCarlo1

plus.google.com/108705527497780816745

amazon.com/author/billydecarlo

goodreads.com/author/show/16887417.Billy_DeCarlo